THE *SHOOTING SCRIPT*®

DAN IN REAL LIFE

THE SHOOTING SCRIPT
DAN IN REAL LIFE

SCREENPLAY WRITTEN BY
PIERCE GARDNER AND PETER HEDGES

INTRODUCTION BY
PIERCE GARDNER

A Newmarket Shooting Script® Series Book
NEWMARKET PRESS • NEW YORK

Screenplay, Motion Picture Artwork, and Photography ™ & © 2007 by Touchstone Pictures

Introduction copyright © 2007 by Pierce Gardner

Q & A with Peter Hedges copyright © 2007 by Rob Feld

All rights reserved. Used by permission.

Grateful acknowledgment to reprint the lyrics to "Let My Love Open the Door" by Peter Townshend, Towser Tunes, Inc. (BMI). All rights o/b/o Towser Tunes, Inc. administered by Songs of Windswept Pacific (BMI).

The Newmarket Shooting Script® Series is a registered trademark of Newmarket Publishing & Communications Company.

This book is published simultaneously in the United States of America and in Canada.

FIRST EDITION

10   9   8   7   6   5   4   3   2   1

ISBN: 978-1-55704-794-6

Library of Congress Catalog-in-Publication Data available upon request.

QUANTITY PURCHASES

Companies, professional groups, clubs, and other organizations may qualify for special terms when ordering quantities of this title. For information, write to Special Sales, Newmarket Press, 18 East 48th Street, New York, NY 10017; call (212) 832-3575 or 1-800-669-3903; FAX (212) 832-3629; or e-mail info@newmarketpress.com.

Website: www.newmarketpress.com

Manufactured in the United States of America.

OTHER BOOKS IN THE NEWMARKET SHOOTING SCRIPT® SERIES INCLUDE:

OTHER NEWMARKET PICTORIAL MOVIEBOOKS AND NEWMARKET INSIDER FILM BOOKS INCLUDE:

CONTENTS

INTRODUCTION

BY PIERCE GARDNER

I began writing *Dan in Real Life* in Sherman Oaks, California, in the summer of 2002.

Only it was called *Dave in Real Life* and it wasn't working. At all.

The problem? Lack of jeopardy.

A year earlier I had started a spec comedy loosely based on my own life. The premise was simple: a married man tries to lure his overachieving wife and kids to the beach for a vacation with his extended family.

To a degree, it mirrored my life. For fifteen years straight, our family had trekked to Rehoboth Beach in Delaware and crammed ourselves into a beach house with my wife's parents *and* my wife's four adult married siblings *and* all their kids.

Twenty-three people in one house, ranging from grandparents to toddlers.

As vacations go, it was like trying to take at nap at the circus. Noisy, crazy, chaotic.

And yet...wonderful.

I was convinced it was a perfect setting for a movie.

And, so far, I was wrong.

Then it hit me.

I had to kill my wife.

I told her at breakfast. I explained that the story was too static. Once they got to the beach, watching characters learn to relax just wasn't that...entertaining.

But...if she was deceased, if my character was a widower, then he could fall in love.

Disastrously. With the absolute wrong person, at the wrong time, right in front of his own daughters and everyone in his extended family.

She frowned. I quickly discovered that wives are less concerned with break-through story concepts than with certain subtle implications.

"You want me...dead?" she said. I nodded. She sighed.

And "Dan" was born.

Now things began to fall into place. Dan had always been a newspaper columnist. But what if he was a "family counselor," a Dr. Phil in print—and could ignore his own good advice? That went in.

What if he had a daughter, just fifteen, who told him she'd fallen in love—in just three days? He could scoff at that—and then tumble into the same trap himself. That went in.

At first Dan had his heart stolen by a stranger, an engaged woman who was getting married that same weekend. I wondered, What would be even worse, even less defendable?

What if...he fell for his brother's girlfriend?

That went in.

Jump to September 2003. Walt Disney had just purchased *Dan in Real Life*. I was elated—and uneasy. Up to now, it had been easy to protect the script. There's a saying, "Every snowflake pleads Not Guilty to the avalanche." To me, this meant, if you make enough small mistakes, you ultimately unleash a catastrophe. Which happens a lot in script development. And *Dan* was a script that many people would be tempted to make "bigger." During the initial writing process, Noah Rosen, my manager, helped keep everything on track with a stream of optimistic encouragement. (This was annoying, as it made it impossible to whine and complain to him.) Noah's partner at the time, Darlene Caamaño Loquet, was equally helpful. But now I was at the mercy of a studio.

But an "avalanche" of bigger, broader changes never happened. My savvy producer, Jon Shestack and his aide, Ginny Brewer, discovered that Disney's

Brad Epstein (who later joined our merry crew) and his boss, Nina Jacobson, saw the same movie. I kept getting good, sensible notes.

But what about the director?

As a teenager, I loved the Stones and the Beatles. How could you not? Is there anything cooler than "Under My Thumb" or "Paperback Writer"? At some point, I dimly noticed their songs were collaborations. With the Stones, it was Jagger-Richards. With the Beatles, you know who.

At the time, it never occurred to me that this process was a big reason the music was so great. Which, of course, it was.

Enter Peter Hedges.

Peter called me in July of 2004. He'd just read the script and come on board. Officially he was just doing a polish, but everyone was hoping that the man who wrote the brilliant movies *What's Eating Gilbert Grape* and *Pieces of April* would join us as our director.

Peter immediately said something interesting. He told me that, for him, the title was a touchstone. It served as a constant reminder that the story needed to stay within the bounds of real human emotion. At that moment, I felt we'd be in good shape. And off he went, to filter *Dan* through his fingertips.

The movie began production in October of 2006. By then, Peter had finished his work, a series of stellar rewrites that had deepened the characters and made the story funnier and more poignant. Now the question was, Would it all come out on film?

When I saw the rough cut in Peter's editing room in New York that February, the answer was "yes." The essence of the story was not only intact; it glowed.

Only now, the story was the product of the two of us.

Which come to think of it, is a Beatles song.

Dan in Real Life

By
Pierce Gardner
And
Peter Hedges

FINAL SHOOTING SCRIPT - 02/08/07

1   INT. DAN'S HOUSE - BEDROOM - EARLY MORNING   1

DAN BURNS, age 42, sleeps. He stirs, instinctively reaching
out his arm for the person next to him. *But no one is there.*

Dan opens his eyes. *Gotta stop doing that.*

The other half of the bed hasn't been slept in for some time.
Books, clothes -- the stuff of life -- are spread out.

Dan sits up. Beat. He takes a deep breath. A new day.

2   INT. DAN'S HOUSE - HOME OFFICE/LAUNDRY ROOM - DAY   2

In the dark, Dan fumbles around, turning on a desk light
which causes him to *squint.*

LATER --

Dan types at a make-shift desk.

From the look of Dan's desk, he could use some help. A pile
of letters addressed to DAN IN REAL LIFE, c/o THE NEW JERSEY
STANDARD. Nearby, a stack of unpaid bills. On the wall,
photos of three girls at various ages. A calendar, opened to
October, each day filled with activities and appointments.

In the background, the clothes dryer BUZZES.

3   INT. DAN'S HOUSE - DINING ROOM - DAY   3

At the dining room table, Dan folds clothes. A girl's tank
top. Another tank top. Then ... *a thong?*

4   INT. DAN'S HOUSE - HALLWAY - DAY   4

Delivering the stacks of laundry, Dan passes his oldest
daughter, JANE BURNS, 17, an old soul, in her robe on her way
to the bathroom.

                    DAN
                (holding up the thong)
          This yours?

                    JANE
          Dad.

                    DAN
          Didn't think so.

                                                      (CONTINUED)

4   CONTINUED: 4

        Dan continues until he comes to a door that is covered with
        photos from magazines and scantily clad pop idols -- the
        cumulative effect is DO NOT DISTURB. MUSIC comes from behind
        the door. Dan sets down a stack of clothes with the thong on
        top and keeps moving toward ...

5   INT. DAN'S HOUSE - LILLY'S ROOM - CONTINUOUS   5

        LILLY BURNS, a heartbreaking 9-year-old, is already dressed
        for the day and carefully packing her small suitcase.

                        DAN
                  Hey, you.
                       (re: the suitcase)
                  I was going to do that for you later.

                        LILLY
                  Now you won't have to.

        She takes the clothes and sets them in a suitcase, near a
        photo of a woman who looks exactly like Lilly, but 25 years
        older.

                        DAN
                  So, kiddo, you hungry? Cereal?

6   INT. DAN'S HOUSE - KITCHEN - DAY   6

        Breakfast is in full swing. Dan pours the milk for Lilly's
        cereal. Jane is loading the dishwasher.

                        DAN
                  So the plan ...

                        JANE
                  The plan ...

        Enter CARA BURNS. She's a 15-year-old girl who seems
        destined to give her father a heart attack. She crosses to
        the refrigerator, yanks open the door and just stares.
        (Note: The back of her low-riding pants should have the
        words YOU WISH written in a rainbow-arc across the rear end.)

                        JANE (CONT'D)
                  Cara, Dad's about to reveal 'the plan.'

                        CARA
                  Oh, great.

                                                          (CONTINUED)

                         DAN
               I'll pack up the car, pick you up right
               after school and then we'll drive
               straight through --

                         LILLY
                    (mouth full with cereal)
               Sounds good.

                         CARA
                    (closes refrigerator door)
               Does not!

                         DAN
               What now?

                         CARA
               Isn't the whole point that we, like, go
               to school, and now you're forcing us to
               miss school, when we should be, like, in
               school?
                    (turning)
               What about my studies?

Dan smiles.

                         CARA
               Why are you smiling?

                         DAN
               I never thought I'd hear you say "What
               about my studies?" It makes me, *like*,
               smile --

                         CARA
                    (exits into dining room)
               I don't wanna go.

                         JANE
               We do this every year.

                         DAN
               It's the only time we can get the whole
               family together.

                         LILLY
               Gotta help Grandma and Grandpa close up
               the house.

Cara reappears in kitchen doorway with her backpack slung
over shoulder. Jane hands her a breakfast bar.

                          DAN
                  (to Cara)
        You, go change.

                        CARA
        I'm not changing.

                        DAN
        Books and newspapers are for reading.
        Your rear-end, however, is not. Go
        change.

Cara looks to Jane for help. But this time no help comes.

                        CARA
                (as she sulks off)
        You're destroying my education.

                        DAN
        I know.

From off, the door bell -- DING DONG.

7   INT. DAN'S HOUSE - FOYER - MOMENTS LATER   7

Dan opens the door to find a lanky TEENAGER with a skull cap.
Jeans almost to his knees. The young man is holding the
morning newspaper, reading the last few lines of Dan's column
-- DAN IN REAL LIFE.

                      TEENAGER
                (a fast talker)
        Very good column, sir. The last bit
        about curfews, very apt. And may I also
        say, sir, that yesterday's column on
        boundary setting, was revelatory ...

                        DAN
        Who are you?

He hands Dan the paper.

                      TEENAGER
        Marty Barasco. Anyway, I especially want
        to thank you for last Friday's column
        because it really helped me understand my
        parents.

                        DAN
                (beat, flattered)
        Well, Marty, what else can I do for you?

>   MARTY
>   I'd like to see your daughter, sir, if I
>   could.
>
>   DAN
>   (happy for Jane)
>   Jane. Jane!
>
>   MARTY
>   Actually, sir, I'm here for Cara.
>
>   DAN
>   (beat)
>   Nice to meet you, Marty. Come back in
>   two years.

Then Dan shuts the door in Marty's face. Beat.

8   EXT. DAN'S HOUSE - LATER   8

A modest house on a modest block. The off-to-school moment.
Dan follows through the doorway as Jane hurries to get Lilly
to the bus stop.

>   JANE
>   ... I don't want to brag but Mr. Schaff
>   says I'm one of the best drivers in the
>   class ... he says that I'm "highway
>   ready"--
>
>   DAN
>   Mr. Schaff and I may not agree. Cara,
>   let's go.
>
>   JANE
>   So will you let me ...?
>
>   DAN
>   We'll see. 3 PM sharp! Do not be --
>
>   JANE
>   We got it, Dad.
>
>   LILLY
>   Yes, we do.
>
>   DAN
>   Late.

Cara follows, her clothes changed. She flips shut her cell
phone, turns and calls back.

8   CONTINUED: 8

                          CARA
                Oh, Dad? FYI, that boy you were really
                rude to before was my *friend* Marty who is
                my lab partner from Science class. We're
                even, like, doing an extra credit project
                together!

So there. She turns, runs to catch up with her sisters.

In the distance, a school bus pulls up.

On Dan, as he watches them go. This sight makes him wistful.

He picks up the empty trash cans and heads back toward the
house.

9   INT. DAN'S HOUSE - DESK - DAY   9

Dan types at his computer, faster than before ...

10   INT. DAN'S HOUSE - KITCHEN - DAY   10

Dan makes a series of individualized sandwiches, assembly-
line style. Nearby a cooler waits to be packed.

11   OMITTED   11

12   EXT. DAN'S HOUSE - DAY   12

Dan forces the last of the suitcases into the back of his car
as his cellphone rings. He answers.

                          DAN
                Hey, Jordy. No, I e-mailed it half an
                hour ago. What?
                     (beat as he gets big news)
                No way. You're kidding.

13   INT. ELEMENTARY SCHOOL - ENTRANCE - DAY   13

Dan bursts through the door and hurries down the hall.

                          DAN
                     (O.S.)
                Sorry I was late.

14   INT. ELEMENTARY SCHOOL - HALLWAY - DAY   14

In the distance, at the end of the hallway, Dan and Lilly are
walking toward us.

                    DAN
          How was your day?

                    LILLY
          Good.

                    DAN
          Me, too. Jordy called and it seems this
          very big columnist -- Andy with the
          Answers is getting the axe -- apparently
          he didn't have the answers anymore ...

A BOY, age 9, passes Lilly and Dan and smiles at Lilly.

                    BOY
          Bye, Lilly.

Lilly smiles back.

Dan looks back at the boy, giving him the proverbial 'hairy
eyeball."

                    DAN
          Anyway -- these people who own a lot of
          newspapers may want me to become him ...

                    LILLY
          Who would be you?

                    DAN
          I'd still be me, but I'd also be him.

In the distance, a WOMAN stops at the water fountain.

                    LILLY
          That's Miss Walker. She's awfully nice.
          And she likes your writing.
          Wave hello.

                    DAN
          I'm waving goodbye to Miss Walker.

15   EXT. HIGH SCHOOL - DAY   15

The Burns family station wagon pulls up to where Jane is
waiting on the steps. She is flanked by TWO FRIENDS. Dan
lowers the passenger window.

                    DAN
          Where's your sister?

                    JANE
          You're late, she went to Yumm's. Can I
          drive?

                    LILLY
               (leaning in from the back seat)
          Dad's going to be syndicated!

                    DAN
          Not so fast. There are two other
          columnists under consideration so --

                    JANE
          That's great. Can I drive?

Dan hesitates, but switches seats. As Jane slides into the
driver's side, her friends let out a cheer.

She adjusts the mirrors, shifts into drive with ease, and
holds the steering wheel in the text-book '10 - 2' position.
Impressive. And then as she drives a short distance
expertly, Dan offers encouragement, "Yes, good." A BOY on a
skateboard crosses, "Watch the kid."

At the school's exit (onto a busy street), Jane carefully
brings the Burns family car to a smooth, confident stop. She
turns on her left turn signal. "Nicely done."

With only one approaching car in the distance, Jane prepares
to accelerate.

                    DAN
          Hold on, hold on. Wait.

Jane could easily have made the turn in time, but she follows
her father's instructions.

                    DAN
          OK, you can go. Go. No, wait.

Another car approaches heading in the other direction.

                                              (CONTINUED)

15   CONTINUED: 15

Jane starts to accelerate, but suddenly - for Dan - it seems
there's traffic coming from all directions. Peril
everywhere!

                    DAN
          Stop. Stop!

Dan is losing it. Then, in a sudden gap in traffic, Dan
shouts:

                    DAN
          OK, you can go. Go!
               (as Jane pulls out)
          No, wait, brakes. Brakes! OK, now go --
          Stop. Now go. Go!

In all the confusion, the car lurches forward into the
intersection, nearly being struck by an SUV heading in one
direction and a school bus full of kids going in the other.
Two other cars have to switch lanes to avoid a collision.

Angle on CHILDREN'S FACES staring down from the school bus at
Jane. *Embarrassing.*

16   EXT. YUMM'S BAKERY - DAY   16

The front grill of the Mercedes as it comes to a stop. PAN
UP to reveal *Dan* driving and Jane, in the passenger seat,
stiff-lipped but upset. Dan kills the engine.

                    DAN
          Look, you're a fine driver. It's just
          the other hundred million drivers that I
          worry about ...

                    JANE
          If you don't let me, I'll never learn --

                    DAN
          But if I let you, you may not live.

Frustrated, Jane bolts out of the car and climbs in the back
seat, passenger side.

                    LILLY
          You got farther than last time.

Dan heads for the door.

17   EXT. YUMM'S BAKERY - CONTINUOUS   17

Dan peers in the first window of Yumm's Bakery. He keeps
moving, peering in every window until he sees ...

A partial view of Cara, in the far corner. Studying? For a
moment, he seems to *melt.* Then the other customers who block
Dan's view move, revealing that Cara is indeed studying ...

The teenaged boy sitting next to her. It's Marty Barasco
from earlier that day.

Dan presses his face against the glass to get a better view.

Cara pulls Marty toward her. They're about to kiss ...

                    DAN
          What the --

Dan POUNDS on the glass with his fists -- WHAP, WHAP, WHAP!

Startled, Cara and Marty -- and the rest of the customers --
turn, giving Dan an instant audience.

Dan stands there, his arms still outstretched above him.
He gestures for Cara to come outside.

Cara looks at him, horrified.

18   EXT. YUMM'S BAKERY - MOMENTS LATER   18

Cara, furious, bursts out of the bakery, Dan holding the
door.

                    CARA
          What was that? What are you doing?!
          Could you be more of an embarrassment?

Dan pulls open the front passenger door for Cara.

                    DAN
          Sorry to interrupt your *studies* with your
          friend.

                    CARA
              (blows past him)
          Well, we can't all be monks like you ...

Dan speaks over the top of the car, as Cara circles around to
sit in the back:

                                                    (CONTINUED)

18   CONTINUED: 18

                    DAN
          By the way, you're grounded.

                    CARA
               (to her sisters)
          I'm grounded. For how long?

                    DAN
               (he shuts the door)
          For life.

                    CARA
               (opens back door)
          What?

                    JANE
               (from inside car)
          Dad, come on ...

                    CARA
               (looks in the back seat, and
                shouts to Jane)
          Humiliating!

                    JANE
          Tell me about it.

                    DAN
               (as he gets in car)
          OK, you're grounded for a month.

                    CARA
          A month! That's worse than forever.
          Why?

                    DAN
          You lied to me.

                    CARA
          Because you can't handle the truth --

                    DAN
          Maybe try me next time --

                    CARA
          OK, Dad, I love Marty.

                    DAN
          Oh, please.

                    CARA
          And I didn't know right away. It took me
          awhile.

                                        (CONTINUED)

                              DAN
                    What's awhile?

                              CARA
                    Well, I've known him three weeks, but I
                    knew in three days.

                              DAN
                         (exploding)
                    Three days? *You can't know in three
                    days.*

Dan tries to start car.

                              JANE
                    Maybe she can.

                              DAN
                    No. No. No. What you're feeling is not
                    love. It's young and reckless and not
                    thought out -- and it may feel like love,
                    but it's not --

The car finally starts and Dan begins to back up.

Cara notices ...

Marty standing forlornly in the closest window of Yumm's.

                              CARA
                         (overlapping, her hands
                          covering her ears)
                    IlovehimIlovehimIlovehim

As the car starts off, Marty tries to keep pace by moving
across the bank of windows, stepping over chairs and around
tables, anything to prolong contact with Cara ...

Angle on Dan and Cara looking at Marty ...

                              CARA
                         (with tears streaming down her
                          face)
                    IlovehimIlovehimIlovehimIlovehim
                    IlovehimIlovehimIlovehimIlovehim
                    IlovehimIlovehimIlovehim ...

Finally, she presses her mouth to the window, KISSING the
glass ...

As the Burns car leaves the frame ...

19   EXT. I-80 EASTBOUND - DAY   19

As the Burns family car takes its place on the fast-moving
and crowded I-80 Eastbound ...

MUSIC. The sound should be big, full, like the world they're
entering.

WIDE ANGLE SHOT of the Burns family car on the New Jersey
Turnpike. How small one car can seem. And then ...

20   OMITTED   20

21   EXT. I-95 - DAY   21

A tense silence in the car as *no one is talking.* Dan, alone,
rides in front. Angle on the three girls in back. Cara is
still upset and angry -- Jane, too, although she has arm
around Lilly who looks around at the others, trying to make
sense of it all.

Meanwhile, out the window, and because *Dan is the slowest
driver on the road,* car after car, truck after truck, whoosh
past ... Lilly counts them.

Jane looks on in disbelief, unaware that on the right, a car
driven by an OLD WOMAN begins to creep past.

                    JANE
                (noticing)
          Oh, great.

Still, Dan, determined, stays the course ...

22   EXT. HIGHWAY GAS STATION / REST STOP - DAY   22

As Dan fills up the car with gas, he stares at the pump.
Nearby, Lilly sits, her head peeking out the window.

                    LILLY
          Dad, you OK?

                    DAN
          There goes Jane's college education.
          There goes Cara's ...

                    LILLY
          Oh, no. What about mine?

                                                    (CONTINUED)

                    DAN
          You're good. Oh, wait. Yep, there it
          goes--

Lilly laughs.

Dan puts back the nozzle, only to find Cara standing next to
the gas pump.

                    CARA
          You can't keep me from Marty. You can
          try, but I want to remind you that *guys
          are half the world*. And I'll find
          others.
                    (with sudden emotion)
          But know that only Marty gets - my -
          heart ...

                    DAN
                    (unfazed)
          In the car.

Cara gets in and as Dan comes around the car, he sees Jane
sitting in the driver's seat.

                    JANE
                    (from inside the car)
          I know a really good driver ...!

                    DAN
          No. No!

23   EXT. CONNECTICUT HIGHWAY - DAY   23

Dan drives.

In the back, Jane listens to her Walkman with headphones.
Cara listens to her Ipod.

Dan reaches into the cooler and hands Lilly a sandwich.
During the following, she takes it out of the baggie and
starts to eat.

                    DAN (CONT'D)
                    (as if it's news)
          I think your sisters aren't very happy
          with me.

                    LILLY
          Duh.

23   CONTINUED: 23

                              DAN
                    Why do you think --

                              LILLY
                    You're a good father, but sometimes
                    you're a bad dad.

Beat. *Ouch.*

                              DAN
                    Hey, who told you to say that?

                              LILLY
                    No one.

                              DAN
                    Was it Jane or Cara? You can tell me.

                              LILLY
                    I made it up myself.

                              DAN
                    No, you didn't. Which one of your
                    sisters --

                              LILLY
                    Dad, I'm in the fourth grade. I can make
                    up things for myself.

                              DAN
                    Jane or Cara -- You can tell me. Jane or
                    Cara?

                              LILLY
                    I'm in the fourth grade, OK? I'm in the
                    fourth grade!

                              JANE AND CARA
                    She's in the fourth grade!

23A   EXT. RHODE ISLAND STATE LINE - DAY   23A

      WHIP PAN as the Burns' car crosses the state line. Camera
      holds on sign which reads ...

                    Welcome to RHODE ISLAND

24   EXT. JAMESTOWN BRIDGE - RHODE ISLAND - MAGIC HOUR   24

      From above, as the Burns' car comes over the bridge. Ocean
      on either side.

25   EXT. ROAD NEXT TO OCEAN - MAGIC HOUR   25

The Burns' car on a road that hugs the shoreline. In the
distance, a LIGHTHOUSE.

                                        MUSIC ENDS AS ...

26   EXT. BEACH HOUSE - NIGHT   26

The Burns' car pulls up at the Burns' family beach house.
Various cars and SUVs are already parked in the circular
driveway. Dan honks twice.

The doors fly open. Teenagers and kids descend on Dan and
his daughters. Jane, Cara and Lilly go inside. Lilly runs
straight into her grandmother's arms. Dan's father -- POPPY -
- approaches.

                    POPPY
          Now we're all here. How you doing?

                    DAN
          Good. Or maybe not. My kids can't stand
          me.

                    POPPY
          Just means you're doing something right.

                    NANA
               (in the doorway, calling up the
                stairs)
          Boys, your brother's here!

27   INT. BEACH HOUSE - CONTINUOUS   27

Dan's mother, NANA greets Dan. Poppy goes past into the
house.

                    NANA
          Dan, your girls. They're all grown up.

                    DAN
          No, no! Not even close. They're still
          very *young*.

Two Girl Cousins -- RACHEL BURNS and OLIVIA WILSON, both 11,
greet the sisters.

The 'Boys' come bounding down the stairs. Meet Dan's
brothers, MITCH and CLAY.

                                        (CONTINUED)

Mitch, the youngest brother, is handsome, tall, buff, in his
mid 30's. The middle brother Clay holds his two-year-old
daughter, JESSICA.

                    MITCH
          Here he is -- Dan the man.

                    DAN
          Hey, guys.
               (regarding the baby)
          Wow, she's ... *big*.

                    CLAY
          And getting bigger.

Dan is almost run over by ELLIOT, age five, who wears pajamas
and who is being pursued by Clay's wife, EILEEN.

                    DAN
          Hey, Eileen.

                    EILEEN
          Hi, Dan. Elliot, bed time!

AMY BURNS, Dan's sister, approaches. Two teenage boys
follow. Amy's son, GUS, is 11. Eileen's son, WILL, is 13.

                    AMY
          You made it.

                    DAN
          Hey, sis.
               (playfully, to nephews)
          Who are you? I don't know you.

                    GUS, THE YOUNGER NEPHEW
          Hi, Uncle Dan.

                    DAN
               (to the older boy)
          And you, say something.

                    WILL, THE OLDER NEPHEW
               (in a post-puberty voice)
          Something.

                    DAN
          Oh wow. It's happened.

Dan and Will, the Older Nephew, high five. HOWARD, Amy's
husband, passes by with BELLA, his eight-year-old daughter
riding piggy back.

                                              (CONTINUED)

>   AMY
>   Help your uncle with his bags ...

Dan starts up the stairs.

>   NANA
>   (from below)
>   Danny, you're down here. Your brother
>   Mitch has a 'friend' coming to visit ...

>   DAN
>   So I get the special room?

>   MITCH
>   Sorry, bro.

>   DAN
>   (smiles)
>   It's OK.

28   INT. BEACH HOUSE - LAUNDRY ROOM - LATER THAT NIGHT   28

The laundry room. An old cot has been wedged in the corner.
It's been made up as a bed. There's a tiny night table
beside it, complete with a lamp and clock radio. Cozy but
cramped.

Dan, in a T-shirt and flannel pajama pants, climbs into the
cot. Gets situated. Just as he's about to turn off the
light, Nana barges in ...

>   NANA
>   Sorry, honey.

Nana quickly transfers the wet towels from the washing
machine to the dryer, turns it on and leaves. The dryer is
surprisingly, actually DEAFENINGLY LOUD.

>   NANA
>   (kissing Dan goodnight)
>   Sleep tight.

Nana exits the room. Dan lies back, reaches up and clicks
off the light.

29   INT. BEACH HOUSE - KITCHEN - DAY   29

Dan emerges from the laundry room to join the early-risers --
Nana, Cara, Jane, Will and Eileen (who feeds Jessica) -- in
the kitchen.

29   CONTINUED: 29

It's a help-yourself breakfast -- bagels, big glass jars
filled full with various cereals, a pitcher of orange juice.
Dan notices Cara and Jane at the counter talking privately to
Nana. Cara appears to be complaining. Jane is supportive.

                         DAN
               Good morning.

Cara won't even look at her dad.

                         DAN
               Sleep well?

As Dan sits down next to her, Cara immediately gets up.

                         DAN
               Can I get you something?

                         CARA
                    (as she goes)
               Get a life.

Beat. Jane follows her.

                         NANA
               She just needs some space.

                         DAN
               That's not what she needs.

                         NANA
               No, she does. From the sound of things,
               you all do.

Beat. Dan watches Eileen as she airplanes a spoonful of
applesauce into Jessica's cooperative mouth.

                         NANA
                    (handing him money)
               Why don't you go get the papers?

                         DAN
               Mom --

                         NANA
               And while you're at it, get lost for a
               little while. It would do you good.

                         DAN
               I should probably (stick around) --

                         NANA
               Get lost, Danny. And it's not a request.

29   CONTINUED: (2)   29

      Dan smiles at his mother. She knows what he needs.

30   EXT. BEACH HOUSE - MORNING   30

      Dan leaves the house -- which is big, old and charming -- and
      heads to his car ...

31   EXT. ROAD WITH ASTONISHING BEACH VIEW - DAY   31

      Dan drives to town. Out his window, the vast Atlantic Ocean.
      In the distance, a lighthouse.

32   EXT. BOOKSTORE - LATER THAT MORNING   32

      In town, a used BOOKSTORE, sits on the edge of the ocean.

      Dan pulls in. He walks over and looks out at the ocean. He
      heads into the store.

33   INT. BOOKSTORE - DAY   33

      Dan enters and grabs two copies of the local newspaper.

      He wanders off into the bookstore.

      LATER --

      With his coat tossed on a step stool, Dan sits among the many
      titles he's taken out.

      As he starts to put back the books he's pulled from the
      shelves, the bell above the front door JINGLES. Dan sees
      that a WOMAN has entered the store.

                          WOMAN (O.S.)
                     (talking to the clerk at the
                      cash register)
                Good morning ...

                          BOOK STORE CLERK (O.S.)
                     (to the customer)
                I'll be with you in a minute.

      Beat. The Woman turns the corner and sees Dan putting the
      last of the books away.

                          WOMAN (O.S.)
                Hi, excuse me, could you help?

                                                         (CONTINUED)

Dan comes down the step ladder.

The Woman Customer. She's striking -- big warm eyes, thick
cascading hair. The sweet upturn of her near perfect nose.

                    DAN
          Yes?

                    WOMAN
          I'm looking for ... a book, obviously.

Dan looks over at the Clerk who is still busy on the phone.

                    DAN
          Anything in particular?

                    WOMAN
          Yes. Something that can help me deal
          with what might be an awkward situation.

                    DAN
          Okay ...

Reticent at first, Dan begins to move down the aisle, and
already he's pulled a book.

                    WOMAN
          Something funny might be nice...

Dan quickly cuts to another aisle.

                    WOMAN (CONT'D)
          But not necessarily big ha ha laugh-out-
          loud funny ... and certainly not make-fun-
          of-other-people funny ...

Dan slows. He's as confused as she is.

                    WOMAN
          But rather something *human* funny --

Dan pulls another book.

                    WOMAN
          And if it could sneak up on you, surprise
          you, and at the same time make you think
          that what you thought was not only right
          in a wrong kind of way, but that when
          you're wrong, there's a certain rightness
          to your wrongness --

What did she say? Dan is moving more quickly now, and the
Woman has to move fast to keep up.

                                              (CONTINUED)

33   CONTINUED: (2)   33

He disappears for a moment, returns with more books, stacking
them on the ever-growing pile which he carries in his arms.

                    WOMAN
          Maybe what I mean is, more importantly
          I'm looking to be swept up and, at the
          same time, *not*, meaning I want to feel a
          deep connection to, uhm, something ...
          Maybe I don't know what I'm looking for.

                    DAN
          In my experience, you rarely ever find it
          all in just one book. Maybe that's why
          there are so many.

                    WOMAN
          So what do we have?

                    DAN
          Oh, just a smattering ... a potpourri of
          possib(ilities)...

                    WOMAN
          Potpourri?

The Woman smiles. Words aren't coming easily for Dan. *Help.*

                    DAN
          Uhm. So ...
               (showing the books)
          Some poetry. Basic stuff. Dickinson.
          A little Neruda is always good.

                    WOMAN
          I agree.

                    DAN
               (moving on to the next book)
          This one, believe it or not, is a page
          turner. *The Biography of Gandhi.* Never
          has anybody been quite so ... cool. What
          else? *A Good Man is Hard to Find.*

                    WOMAN
          The title alone.

                    DAN
               (surprised it made into the
                stack)
          Anna Karenina?

                    WOMAN
               (making a joke)
          Now that's funny.

                                              (CONTINUED)

                              DAN
                    No, funny's coming.

He holds up the children's book - *Everyone Poops.*

An awkward beat.

                              DAN
                    OK, maybe it's not funny.

                              WOMAN
                    No, actually, that's funny.
                         (laughing)
                    Very funny. And true.

                              DAN
                    Good. Good.

Beat as Dan just stares at her, lost in the moment.

                              WOMAN
                    But if you could pick only one ...

                              DAN
                         (not taking his eyes off her)
                    Well, no book in my mind rivals ...
                         (holding up the book)
                    The Romance of Fish Life.

Woman laughs.

                              DAN
                    The truth is I just started grabbing
                    whatever I could ... grab.

The Clerk, finally off the phone, appears, breaking the
moment.

                              CLERK
                    So, ma'am, you were looking for --

                              MARIE
                    Sold.

                              CLERK
                    I'm sorry?

                              MARIE
                    I want them all.

Confused, the Clerk notices the tall stack of books.

                              DAN
                No, no, these were just suggestions --

Marie hands the clerk the books.

                              MARIE
                         (to Clerk)
                And you'll make sure he gets the
                commission for this?

                              CLERK
                He doesn't work here.

Beat. The Woman looks at Dan, who shrugs slightly. Busted.

                              MARIE
                         (to Clerk)
                Well, he should.
                         (to Dan)
                You're smooth.

                              DAN
                         (surprising himself)
                No, actually I'm not, uhm, smooth. I'm
                Dan.
                         (beat)
                Sorry.

The Woman extends her hand.

                              MARIE
                Marie.

His arm full with books, Dan manages to extend a hand and
they shake.

                              DAN
                So, Marie, can I make it up to you?

34   INT. FERRY WAITING ROOM - OFF SEASON - DAY   34

Dan brings tea and a muffin to where Marie sits.

                              DAN
                Here we go. Your tea. Hot. My juice.
                I asked for a muffin, but it appears they
                gave us a small planet.

He takes a seat across from Marie.

                    DAN
I brought napkins and utensils. I'm a
big believer in forks.

Marie tears off a chunk with her fingers.

                DAN (CONT'D)
And apparently you are not.

                  MARIE
So, Dan, you were born.

Beat. Dan hesitates. (Which is a good thing because this is
the last pause he will take for some time.)

                    DAN
Yes, I was born, like everybody else, and
I grew up, like everybody else ...

Marie takes her first bite of muffin.

                    DAN
Is it good?

Her mouth full, Marie gestures that it's good but she wants
Dan to keep talking.

                    DAN
And what else? OK, I went to school, and
I had a Bonanza lunch pail ...

                    OVER A SERIES OF DISSOLVES:

                    DAN
Then I wanted to be a magician.
I staged my own show where I tried to
make the neighbor girl float ... and she
didn't float ... needless to say it
involved a plaster cast and some stitches
and that was the end ... of my magic
career ...

                    DISSOLVE TO:

Dan and Marie laughing.

                    DAN
And I've never told anyone this before...

                    DISSOLVE TO:

(CONTINUED)

                              DAN
                    So I was the RA for the dorm -- that's a
                    Resident Assistant -- and she was the
                    freshman with the loud stereo.
                         (said quickly, off-handedly)
                    And then it was good and the girls came
                    and then it got even better and then she
                    got sick and we lost her and it's taken
                    us some time ...

Marie yanks a napkin out of the dispenser.

                              DAN
                         (beat, sees Marie is upset)
                    And I think we should talk about
                    something else ...

                              MARIE
                         (dabbing her eyes)
                    So you're telling me that you're one-of-
                    those-widowers-with-three-daughters-who-
                    preys-on-unsuspecting-women-in-book-
                    stores ...

                              DAN
                    That, it seems, would be me.

                              MARIE
                    Been there!

                              DAN
                    Really?

                              MARIE
                    No. Seriously. It sounds like it's been
                    hard.

                              DAN
                    We're all OK now. We really are ...

                              MARIE
                    You don't have to smile.

                              DAN
                    It's better than the alternative.

Marie's cell phone rings.

                              MARIE
                    Excuse me.
                         (beat, answers)
                    Hi.   No, I'm minutes away.
                         (MORE)

(CONTINUED)

34 CONTINUED: (3)   34

                              MARIE (cont'd)
                         (hangs up)
                    I've gotta go.

35 EXT. FERRY WAITING ROOM - MOMENTS LATER   35

    Marie, in-a-hurry, heads to her car. Dan follows, carrying
    the books.

                              MARIE
                    I just lost track of time --

                              DAN
                    I wish we could keep talking --

                              MARIE
                    Well, it was nice -- and a bit unusual -
                    meeting you --

                              DAN
                    Maybe I could call you sometime?

    Marie closes the trunk and turns to him.

                              MARIE
                    That might be awkward.

                              DAN
                    Because you're in a relationship.

                              MARIE
                    Yes -- a new one.

                              DAN
                    Something I would've found out if I
                    hadn't been doing all the talking.

                              MARIE
                         (because it is)
                    True, but --

                              DAN
                    But it's not exactly fair, is it? That
                    you know all about me and I know nothing
                    about you.
                         (beat)
                    Look, I don't want to go through the rest
                    of my life wondering about the woman in
                    the bookstore who let me do all the
                    talking. All we'd be is just two people
                    finishing a conversation --

                              MARIE
                    OK, no harm in that ...

                                                        (CONTINUED)

Marie writes her number on the back of the bookstore receipt.

                    MARIE
               (as she writes)
        Call, or don't. But call.

She hands Dan her number. Then starts her car.

                    DAN
        I will.

As she starts to drive off, Dan impulsively knocks on her
window.

                    DAN
        Just so you know -- I would even call to
        say I'm not calling!

Marie drives off and Dan watches her go.

36   EXT. DOWNTOWN - DAY   36

Dan drives, his thoughts racing.

                    DAN
        "I'd even call to say I'm not calling."
        Wow, that's brilliant.

Absorbed in his thoughts, Dan sails through a stop sign.
A HORN BLARES, a passing car swerves.

                  DAN (CONT'D)
        Sorry, sorry, sorry!

A cop siren SOUNDS.

37   EXT. STREET - DAY   37

Dan has his license handed back to him by a local POLICEMAN,
poker-faced, severe.

                    DAN
        I never do this kind of thing, Officer.
        I'm usually so ... careful ... and no one
        believes in rules more than --

The Policeman grunts. He's heard it all before.

                  DAN (CONT'D)
        It's just not like me ...

(CONTINUED)

37   CONTINUED: 37

The Policeman tears off the ticket and hands it to him.

                    POLICEMAN
          Welcome to Rhode Island.

The Policeman walks away.

                    DAN
          Thank you. It's -- nice to be here.

38   INT. BEACH HOUSE - VESTIBULE - DAY   38

Poppy, in the middle of yet another close-up-the-house-for-
the-year project (this one involves a small ladder), notices
as...

Dan enters the house, with newspapers tucked under an arm.

                    POPPY
          What's wrong?

                    DAN
               (startled)
          Nobody. I mean, nothing.

                    POPPY
               (calling out)
          Danny's back!

Poppy takes the newspapers, then disappears into the house,
passing Mitch and Clay who stop, take in Dan who doesn't seem
his usual self.

                    MITCH
          Dude, you all right?

                    DAN
          Yes, no. I'm good, I'm good.

                    CLAY
          Really? You don't seem good.

                    DAN
               (crossing to them in the living
                room)
          Well, it was the strangest thing. I --
          Uhm -- Wow.

                    CLAY
          Wow what?

                                              (CONTINUED)

                        DAN
                    (secretively)
          I met someone. And she was really
          something.

                        CLAY
          Hot damn.

                        MITCH
          Bro, this is beyond huge. Did you get
          her number?

                        DAN
          Yes, but --

                        CLAY
          You gonna call?

                        DAN
          It's complicated --

                        MITCH
          It's simple. You gotta call.

                        CLAY
          He just met her, he's probably worried
          it's too soon.

                        MITCH
          It's never too soon, a guy his age.

                        DAN
          No, it's that --

Amy, passing through --

                        CLAY
          Amy, Dan met someone!

                        DAN
          Shhh!

                        AMY
          You met someone?

                        DAN
          Shhhh, please!

Eileen appears.

                        HOWARD
          Dan met someone?

                                          (CONTINUED)

>   CLAY
>   Eileen, honey, how soon till he can call?

>   EILEEN
>   How would I know? I haven't been single
>   for *ages*.

>   AMY
>   Me neither. Ohmigod, who is she?

Cousins Will, Gus, Rachel (holding Jessica) and Olivia appear
in the background -- and one of them, Rachel, the loudest of
the loud, calls out -- "Did Uncle Dan meet someone?!"

>   MITCH
>   Yes, kids, he met a hottie.

Dan is flustered.

>   DAN
>   OK, that's enough, please ...

>   MITCH
>   You know what? Let's ask Annie.

Angle on Dan. *Annie? Who's Annie?* He turns as Annie comes
down the stairs. Annie looks exactly like Marie from the
bookstore, because she *is* Marie from the bookstore.

>   MITCH
>   (to Annie)
>   There's something we want to ask you.

Dan freezes. *No, it can't be her. This can't be happening.*

>   ANNIE
>   What's the ...
>   (sees Dan)
>   ... question?

>   MITCH
>   Annie, this is my brother Dan. He could
>   use your advice. He just met some hottie
>   in town and ...
>   (beat)
>   Annie's a little shell-shocked.

>   CLAY
>   Why wouldn't she be? Mitch neglected to
>   mention that in their weekend away, she'd
>   be meeting our entire family.

>   MITCH
>   I didn't want to scare her off.
>
>   NANA
>   Let's go people! Let's go!
>
>   DAN
>   Annie, is it?

The Others begin to disperse.

>   MARIE
>   It's Anne-Marie. Mitch calls me Annie;
>   I'm Marie everywhere else.
>
>   MITCH
>   (nuzzling her)
>   I already had two Marys and a Martha in
>   my exercise class; I didn't want people
>   getting confused.
>
>   DAN
>   (still confused)
>   No, that wouldn't be good.
>
>   MARIE
>   I prefer Marie.

Awkward beat. There's so much more to say that can't be
said.

>   NANA
>   C'mon sweetie, the women are on the
>   porch.

39   EXT. BEACH HOUSE - PORCH - MINUTES LATER   39

Nana, Eileen and Amy have been joined by all the other
females who can read. This includes Jane, Cara and Lilly.
And the distracted newcomer, Marie.

Amy, bright and funny, is the grand-mistress of ceremonies.

>   AMY
>   All that remains, seven letters, starts
>   with 'c.'
>
>   JANE
>   Carcass.

39   CONTINUED: 39

Marie is still shaken from her reunion with Dan, but somehow
she manages ...

                    MARIE
          Cadaver.

                    AMY
          Perfect. Briefest time units, four
          letters.

                    EILEEN
          Mili.

                    MARIE
          Nano.

Cara sees Elliot eavesdropping at the door.

                    CARA
          Hey -- no spying!

Squealing, Elliot across the family room toward the ...

40   INT. BEACH HOUSE - STUDY - CONTINUOUS   40

The male family members in a scene of thinly-veiled
desperation.

HOWARD, Amy's Husband, is doing his best to lead the troops.

                    ELLIOT
          You guys are way behind!

                    HOWARD
          That's not helping.

                    POPPY
          I don't think 'secretive' fits.

From where he sits, by leaning slightly forward, Dan can
glimpse Marie on the porch.

                    HOWARD
          No, it doesn't fit. Let's go on to 12
          Across.

                    POPPY
          We're moving on.

                                            (CONTINUED)

40   CONTINUED: 40

                         CLAY
                    (whispering)
          For you to be interested in someone. She
          must be special.

                         HOWARD
                    (the clue is too daunting)
          Let's skip 12 Across.

                         DAN
          This is what I'm trying to tell you --
          it's not going to happen. She's already
          dating someone.

                         MITCH
          That's not your problem, bro.

                         DAN
          Actually, it kind of is.

                         HOWARD
          Listen up! 15 Across. 5 letter word for
          Pan-Fry.

                         POPPY
          Pan-fry, let's go.

                         MITCH
          Dude, is there a rock on her left hand?

                         DAN
          Not yet, but --

                         MITCH
          Then all's fair.

     ON DAN: *No, I don't think so.*

                         POPPY (O.C.)
          Focus, people! Pan-fry!

41   EXT. BEACH HOUSE - PORCH - DAY   41

     ON MARIE:

                         MARIE
               Saute.

                         AMY
          Yes!

                                              (CONTINUED)

> MARIE
> And the word before, did we try
> *Zeitgeist*?

> AMY
> Ohmigod.

> MARIE
> Which I think then would make *ozone* work?

> EILEEN
> Oh, lordy, it seems we've hit the mother
> lode!

Lilly giggles. Marie is her new hero.

ANGLE ON Nana and the girls as they take in Marie. This is
some woman.

> AMY
> 10 Letters. Anything that can go wrong,
> will.
> (turning to Marie)
> So...

42 INT. BEACH HOUSE - STUDY - MOMENTS LATER   42

The Men/Boys are struggling.

> MITCH
> Baked? Try baked.

> POPPY
> You gotta be kidding. *Baked* for Pan-Fry?

> CLAY
> Dan. Earth to Dan.

> DAN
> (looking in the direction of
> the porch)
> Huh?

> CLAY
> We're still at Across. We're not even at
> Down, Dan. We're not even at Down.

> MITCH
> We're dying here, buddy. We're...

The Women let out a cheer from the other room.

(CONTINUED)

                    POPPY
          We're done.

43   INT. BEACH HOUSE - KITCHEN - DAY   43

Dan, Clay and Mitch scrub dishes and clean up. Poppy and
Howard clear the table. The Boys help, too.

                    CLAY
          Dan! What happened to you? You were
          useless.

                    DAN
          Sorry, guys ...

                    MITCH
          Lay off him! He's got other things on
          his mind.

                    HOWARD
               (softly)
          Saute.

Nana passes through the kitchen.

                    MITCH
          Mom, Dad? Whaddya think of ... (Marie)?

                    POPPY
          Mitchell, it's too early to tell.

                    NANA
          That said, she's bright. Lovely.
          Adorable. And if you botch this up,
          we'll keep her and get rid of you.

Beat. Mitch smiles.

                    NANA
               (as she goes)
          And Dan, honey, you missed a spot.

Mitch sidles up to Dan who continues with the dishes.

                    MITCH
          What do you think?

                    DAN
          She's ... great.

HOLD ON Dan as Mitch turns away, satisfied, throws his dish
towel on the counter.

44   INT. BEACH HOUSE - UPSTAIRS HALLWAY - DAY   44

Dan comes up the stairs, looking toward Marie's open door ...

From inside her room, Marie looks out. (Something about this
should suggest they've both been looking for an opportunity
to talk.)

As Dan and Marie move toward each other, Rachel and Elliot
giggle as they run past. A game of hide n' seek is about to
be played in the house, so kids are running every which way.

                    DAN
         WOULD YOU LIKE TO KNOW WHERE WE ARE?

                    MARIE
         Yes. YES.

                    DAN
              (finger across the map,
               whispers)
         Look, if I had known, I never would've --
         not my brother's girlfr(iend) --

                    MARIE
         Of course not --

                    DAN
         And, for the record, I never called you a
         hottie --
              (as Clay comes up the stairs
               with Jessica)
         OH, HERE WE ARE. SEE, WE'RE ON THE BAY
         SIDE.

                    MARIE
         OH, I SEE.

                    DAN
         What should we do?

                    MARIE
         It is kind of funny. Maybe we should
         just tell everyone.

                    DAN
         No. No no no no no.

                    MARIE
         We didn't do anything wrong. It was
         sweet --

                                              (CONTINUED)

Cara sulks past, clutching her cell phone.

>   DAN
>   AND THE OCEAN IS CLOSE.   IT'S HERE.

>   MARIE
>   OH, I SEE.

>   MITCH
>   (comes around the corner)
>   Oh, good, you guys getting to know each
>   other?

Dan and Marie turn, startled.

>   DAN
>   Just showing her where we are on the map.

>   MITCH
>   Thanks, bro.

>   WILL (O.S.)
>   Uncle Mitch, you're not counting.

>   MITCH
>   Oh, right.
>   (to Dan and Marie)
>   Hey, you two better hide.

Mitch turns away, covers his eyes and begins to count.

44A   INT. UPSTAIRS HALLWAY - MOMENTS LATER   44A

Bella and Lilly run down the hall -- they split off, Lilly
into the girls' room and Bella (who we follow) runs into Nana
and Poppy's room.

45   INT. NANA AND POPPY'S ROOM - CONTINUOUS   45

Bella passes Dan and Marie, crouching in the corner, a
respectable distance between them. In terms of hiding, it's
the best they could do. Bella pulls open a closet door and
before disappearing inside, says:

>   BELLA
>   I see you.

Dan and Marie sink lower. In the background, Will, Olivia
and Gus scatter in all direction as ...

Mitch, from down below, counts in a very Mitch-like way
throughout the scene. "21, Twenty-TWOOOOOOO, Twenty-
THREEEEEEE!"

                    DAN
          Mitch is a great guy.

                    MARIE
          He is. He's fun. And funny.
          Uncomplicated, in the good way. Just
          what I need.

                    DAN
          He's a great guy.

                    MARIE
          See, I just ended this long, messy
          relationship, and I joined this gym, and
          Mitch was there ...

                    DAN
          He's a great guy.

                    MARIE
          You keep saying that.

                    DAN
          Well, because he is.
               (beat)
          So good luck --

Beat. Marie is taken aback by Dan's abruptness. Then a pack
of kids come racing through the room, and the last kid,
perhaps Lilly, pulls Marie along, leaving Dan alone ...

                    DAN
               (to himself)
          -- to all of us.

                    MITCH (O.S.)
          44 - 45 - 50-75-100-ReadyornotHereICome!

46   EXT. BEACH - DAY - MAGIC HOUR   46

Waves CRASH on the rocks as the Burns family walks the beach.

The kids are out front, running ahead, looking for shells,
driftwood. Marie surrounded by Mitch and a cluster of the
adults follow. It's all very polite, but Marie is in the
middle of being grilled. Dan and Poppy trail behind.

                                              (CONTINUED)

                    POPPY
          So a little bird told me you're going to
          be syndicated ...

                    DAN
          Lilly. They're looking at a bunch of
          columnists. It's a long shot, at best --

Jane drops back to update Dan and Poppy.

                    JANE
          She's amazing. Name a place, she's
          either lived there or visited. Tibet.
          Chile. Berlin when there was the wall.

From the group in front, there's laughter and Jane calls out:

                    JANE
               (rejoining the group)
          Wait, what did I miss?

Beat. Dan strains to hear what's up ahead. But it's
useless.

                    POPPY
          Well, Mitch certainly made out.

                    DAN
          Yep.

                    POPPY
          What about you? Have you found anyone?

                    DAN
          Dad, don't --

                    POPPY
          Look, I know you always say that with
          Suzanne you won the lottery. And that to
          try again would feel greedy. But it's
          been four years --

                    DAN
          Can we just walk? Please.

Beat. As they continue to walk.

WIDE SHOT: The entire family, wrapped in heavy jackets and
scarves, is walking the beach. Some kids have run ahead and
are starting to climb up the empty life guard chair.

47   INT. BEACH HOUSE - DINING ROOM - NIGHT   47

Marie -- candlelit -- sits in the middle of a long table,
surrounded by the large Burns family.

                    EILEEN
          How did you two meet?

                    MARIE
          I was at the gym and I had just finished
          running on the treadmill ... and there
          was this man (your uncle) standing in
          front of me ... and he was cute in a very
          sweaty way ... and then he sneezed ...

                    MITCH
          Truth be told, I snarted.

                    NANA
          You what?

                    MITCH
          Snarted. You know, the sneeze/fart
          combination.

                    DAN
          Must we.

                    MARIE
          He took me by the arm and pulled me out
          of the way.

                    MITCH
          I was trying to spare you.

                    MARIE
          And I never smelled a thing.

Everyone laughs, but no one laughs like Marie. Her laugh is
generous -- full-bodied -- infectious.

                    DAN
          Corn. Somebody please pass the corn.
               (sees the bowl of corn right in
                front of him)
          Oh. Got it. Got it.

                    MARIE
          So that's how we met.

                    MITCH
          Can I just say my version of it?

                    AMY
          No, Mitch --

                    CARA
          What's your sign?

                    MARIE
          Scorpio, Libra rising.

                    CARA
          Ohmigod. So am I.

                    JANE
          Do you have any siblings?

                    MARIE
          No.

                    DAN
               (faintly)
          Who wants corn?

                    HOWARD
          And where do you work?

                    CARA
               (at the same time as Howard)
          What's your favorite color?

                    MARIE
          Blue. I've had lots of different jobs
          but ... right now I run a small graphic
          design company in the city ... I also
          like orange.

                    EILEEN
          Tell us something about yourself that few
          people know, not even Mitch.

                    MARIE
               (beat, leans forward, a secret)
          I am an accomplished maker of pancakes.

                    CLAY
          Talent Show. Talent Show.

                    AMY
          What would your perfect day be?

                    MITCH
          Mine would start with Annie. It would
          end with Annie --

                                      (CONTINUED)

47   CONTINUED: (2)   47

                         AMY
                    (trying to interrupt)
               Mitch! Once again, we're not asking you.
                    (back to Marie)
               So you were saying?

                         MARIE
               My perfect day would start with going to
               a country where they speak a language I
               don't know, new customs, some place where
               I'm completely out of my element...

                         POPPY
               Welcome. I think you've arrived ...

     The family, except for Dan, laughs.

                         MITCH
               I JUST WANT TO SAY -- WHEN I SAW HER THAT
               FIRST TIME, I THOUGHT TO MYSELF --

                         NANA
               Honey, you don't have to shout.

                         MITCH
                    (beat, softly, from the heart)
               I thought to myself -- Did I just die?
               Because there's an angel in the room.

     Beat. A collective "AWWWW."

     On Dan as he stares awe-struck at the 'angel' in the room.

48   INT. BEACH HOUSE - KITCHEN - NIGHT   48

     Dan yanks open the refrigerator's freezer door and quickly
     inhales the cold air.

     He moves down the counter where TWO PIES sit out for dessert.
     He jerks open various drawers, digging around for something,
     then he grabs and draws back a BIG KNIFE and stabs one of the
     pies.

     Then he realizes a kitchen table full of his nieces and
     nephews and Lilly have all stopped and watch him, speechless.

     Dan smiles, knowing how ridiculous he must look. And then...

49   INT. BEACH HOUSE - DINING ROOM - NIGHT   49

Dan enters the room, balancing the two pies. One has the
knife stuck in the middle.

                    DAN
          Dessert!

                    POPPY
               (quietly)
          Danny, some of us are still eating.

                    DAN
          It's getting late.

                    JANE
               (next to Poppy)
          No, it's not.

                    DAN
          Well, it feels late. Here.

Dan sets down the pies on the table and begins to slice a
first piece.

Meanwhile, at the other end of the table, Marie pauses to
take a much deserved bite of food and the others pounce.

There's barely a beat before Cara, Howard and Nana all start
to ask Marie a question at the same time. As they try to
sort out who should go first, Clay blurts out --

                    EILEEN
          I was an only child, too, this must be
          pretty overwhelming --

                    HOWARD
          Have you ever lived your perfect day?

                    CARA
          So at what point does your boyfriend
          become your lover?

Before Marie can answer, Dan blurts out --

                    DAN
          OK, everybody, I think we can stop with
          the questions. You've been grilling her
          all night.

                                              (CONTINUED)

> NANA
> I'm sorry, does it feel like we're
> grilling?

> MARIE
> No, not at all --

> DAN
> She's just being nice --

> MARIE
> No, I like the questions --

> DAN
> Puh-lease. On behalf of my family, I
> want to apologize. None of Mitch's
> previous girlfriends have been subjected
> to such in-depth questioning

> CLAY
> Dan does have a point.

> DAN
> - not the body double, or that Knicks'
> City Dancer, and certainly none of the
> flight attendants from every major and
> regional airline who have wheeled their
> carts through this very house.

> POPPY
> OK, enough.

> DAN
> What? I mean, am I wrong? Is this not
> true?

A tense silence. Then ...

> MITCH
> Wow, Dan. Thank you for pointing that
> out.
>   (means it)
> You're the smartest guy I know.

Beat. 'Ouch' for Dan.

> MITCH
> And you're right. It's Annie's turn to
> ask me whatever -

>   DAN
>   (under his breath, can't help
>   himself)
>   She prefers Marie.

Beat. All eyes turn to Marie.

>   MITCH
>   Ask me whatever you want, *Marie.*

>   MARIE
>   I don't have any questions.

>   DAN
>   Oh, come on.

>   JANE
>   *Dad.*

>   MARIE
>   Mitch said early on that if I'd forgive
>   him his past, he'd forgive me mine.

Beat. *Wow.*

>   DAN
>   Well, that's a stupid thing to do.

Dan takes a first bite of pie.

Nana, embarrassed by Dan's behavior, stands suddenly and
says:

>   NANA
>   (with a false cheeriness)
>   OK, everyone into the family room and,
>   John, bring the pies.
>   (under her breath to Dan)
>   Not you. You'll be doing the dishes.
>   Alone.

50   INT. BEACH HOUSE - KITCHEN - HALF AN HOUR LATER   50

Dan is mid-way through washing a stack of plates.

Off screen, in the family room, everyone else plays charades.
There's laughter, cheering and the calling out of clues.

Dan takes a plate off the stack only to find Mitch standing
before him, picking up a towel, ready to help.

(CONTINUED)

>   DAN
>   Hey, I'm sorry. I was way, way out of
>   line --

>   MITCH
>   No, you're never out of line. You're my
>   brother ...

>   DAN
>   Yes, but I think you'll understand when I
>   tell you --

>   MITCH
>   Listen, bro: There's nothing you could
>   do or say that would upset me.

>   DAN
>   But the woman I met before at the
>   bookstore --

>   MITCH
>   (Over Dan)
>   Wait, can I just say one thing?
>   (Beat)
>   When you were talking about all my other
>   girls, I realized something. What I feel
>   for Marie is ... *different*.

Mitch looks toward the family room. Dan looks, too.

Dan's POV: From this angle, Marie can be seen through the
doorway taking her turn, acting out a charade.

>   MITCH
>   You know that feeling when your ...

Mitch unconsciously touches his chest.

>   DAN
>   Heart ...

>   MITCH
>   When your heart is ...

>   DAN
>   Pounding ...

>   MITCH
>   Yes ...

>   DAN
>   ... like it's actually outside your
>   ribs ...

                      MITCH
         Yep.

                      DAN
         Exposed - vulnerable - no protection ...

                      MITCH
         Yes ...

                      DAN
         And you feel wonderful and awful and
         heartsick and alive all at the same time.

                      MITCH
         Yes! What do we call that?

                      DAN
         Oh - love.

                      MITCH
         You always did have the words.

A cheer comes from the other room as Marie's charade has been
guessed. Mitch goes to her. Alone, Dan watches for a
moment. Then he turns away and starts to *bang - bang - bang*
his head into the nearest wall.

51   INT. BEACH HOUSE - GIRL'S ROOM - NIGHT   51

It's bedtime. Jane is talking colleges with Amy. Rachel and
Olivia are getting their beds ready. Lilly and Bella are in
their pajamas.

                      JANE
         Stanford or Berkeley...

                      AMY
         Those are great schools.

                      JANE
         Maybe the University of Washington ...

Dan sticks his head in the door.

                    JANE (CONT'D)
                 (more for Dan)
         Or somewhere closer to home.

An awkward beat.

                         DAN
           Lil', if you can't sleep, you know where
           to find me.

                         LILLY
                   Dad.

Instead, Lilly goes into the bathroom as Cara comes out.

She looks past Dan, out into the hall where Mitch is
searching the bookcase. Around him, the others bustle about
getting ready for bed.

                         CARA
                   (calling past Dan)
           Uncle Mitch, are you going in for your
           good night kiss?

51A   INT. BEACH HOUSE - UPSTAIRS HALLWAY - CONTINUOUS   51A

Dan looks back over his shoulder ...

                         MITCH
           You bet.

Clay is behind Mitch. Eileen and Elliott, too.

                         CLAY
           Ah, yes, Mom and Dad's old separate-
           bedrooms-if-you're-not-married rule.

                         EILEEN
           It is kind of High School.

                         DAN
           Oh, I agree with that rule.

                         POPPY
                   (from his bedroom)
           Thank you, Dan.

                         DAN
           You're welcome.

                         AMY
                   (crossing out of the girl's
                    room)
           Mitch, what are you doing?

                    MITCH
Marie brought all these books and I think
she should read a real book by a real
writer.

Mitch pulls out a copy of Dan's novel -- *The Lost Pages*.

                    DAN
That's not a good idea --

                    MITCH
Au contraire.

                    DAN
Please don't --

                    MITCH
It's the best book I've ever read.

                    AMY
It may be the only book you've ever read.

                    POPPY
Be nice.

                    MITCH
Funny.
          (extending a pen)
And if you could sign it, I think it
would mean a lot.

Dan hesitates ... then starts to sign.

                    NANA
Careful -- that's a first edition ...

                    DAN
It's the only edition.

Nana kisses the boys goodnight.

                    MITCH
          (reading what Dan wrote)
"Good luck?" That's it?
          (beat)
Well, OK, we can work with that.

Mitch knocks lightly and then disappears into Marie's room.
The door closes. As do all the other doors to all the other
rooms.

Beat.

51A   CONTINUED: (2)   51A

                                DAN
                           (not moving)
                    Good-night.

Beat.

Then Dan exits the frame.

52   INT. BEACH HOUSE - LAUNDRY ROOM/DAN'S ROOM - DAY   52

A slant of morning light cuts across the room as Dan wakes
up.

52A   INT. BEACH HOUSE - KITCHEN - DAY   52A

Dan emerges from his room ...

Poppy and Jessica are having some quality time alone in the
kitchen.

                                POPPY
                    Can you say good morning?

                                JESSICA
                    Morning.

Dan pours himself a cup of coffee.

                                POPPY
                           (to Dan)
                    Have fun.

53   EXT. BEACH HOUSE - PORCH AND YARD - MOMENTS LATER   53

Dan comes out of the house onto the porch passing Nana and
Howard who are doing the crossword puzzle ...

                                NANA
                           (to Dan, as he passes)
                    5 letter word for desire ...

Dan stops, sees Marie, lying on the porch, stretching and
reading Dan's novel *The Lost Pages*.

                                DAN
                           (laughs)
                    I don't know.

                                              (CONTINUED)

In the back yard, Mitch is preparing to lead an exercise
class.

> MITCH
> Marie! We're starting! Mom? Will you
> hit the music?

Howard and Marie head down the stairs.

Nana exits into the house.

Then Clay appears from behind, dragging Dan along.

> CLAY
> C'mon, Bro. You need it more than I do.

As Clay and Dan join the others, MUSIC starts.

Mitch calls out the routine:

> MITCH
> Boxer shuffle!

The group follows him.

> MITCH
> Knees!

Alternating knee kicks ensue.

> MITCH
> Shuffle...Jab left...right...

Marie takes off her zip-up as Mitch switches to speedbag.

> MITCH
> Jump rope!

Mitch then encourages Marie to take the lead. She
demonstrates a 'salsa-esque' move.

> MITCH
> Beginners in the middle.

Mitch moves Dan into position directly behind Marie. Mitch
moves on to help others.

Marie's moves are far more creative and hard to follow.
There's clearly a dancer in her. People try to reach and
swing and bend to her lead.

(CONTINUED)

53   CONTINUED: (2)   53

                          MITCH
              Listen, everyone. Marie. An example of
              what to do. Dan. An example of what not
              to do.

53B   OMITTED   53B

54   EXT. BEACH HOUSE - YARD - LATER   54

Work-out over, the group applauds, then disperses.

                          OLIVIA
              Thanks, Uncle Mitch.

                          RACHEL
              Way better than last year's.

                          CLAY
              Whoo! I feel good!

Dan comes up the porch steps, then looks back at ...

Mitch who says to Marie ...

                          MITCH
                    (indicating his thighs)
              I'm a little stiff.

Mitch and Marie face each other with their legs spread,
holding each other's elbows, Mitch leans back, which pulls
Marie forward.

From Dan's POV - it appears - what with the bouncing and the
proximity of Marie's head to Mitch's crotch - to be something
more than just stretching.

Dan does an about face and addresses the newly arrived Lilly.

                          DAN
              Get your sisters and meet me out front.
              Get 'em now. Now!

55   EXT. BEACH HOUSE - MOMENTS LATER   55

Outside, Dan paces. Then turns, sees ...

Two kids -- Bella and Elliot -- standing with their fleeces
on, looking hopeful.

                                                    (CONTINUED)

                              BELLA
                    Where are you going? Can we come with?

                              ELLIOT
                    Can we, can we, can we?

                              DAN
                    Actually, my girls are needing some
                    family time, some quality alone time with
                    their dad. So how about we do it next
                    time.

Always the good sport, Lilly is the first out on the porch,
ready to go.

                              DAN
                    In the car.
                         (calling from the yard)
                    Cara, Jane -- let's go!

Jane and Cara come out onto the porch.

                              JANE
                    What is it, Dad? Nana's going to teach
                    me how to knit.

Jane goes back inside.

                              DAN
                    Cara, let's go.

                              CARA
                    No!

This leaves Dan with just Lilly. He eyes Bella and Elliot.

                              DAN
                    So, come on, what are you waiting for?

Bella and Elliot appear confused. *Can they trust this man?*

ANGLE ON MARIE, watching from a window.

MARIE'S POV: As Dan gets a booster seat from Clay's SUV and
makes sure the three kids are safely buckled up.

From off, Mitch can be heard saying, "Marie, want to go for a
run."

As the car pulls out, Marie turns away.

56   EXT. SHACK O' SHELLS - A TOURIST ESTABLISHMENT - DAY   56

They pull up at a touristy gift shop.

ON DAN. *Something's not right.*

Dan and the kids get out of the car. Somewhat stunned, Dan
stares through the soaped-over windows of the now closed (and
empty) SHACK O' SHELLS.

                    DAN
          Oh, man. No. No, it can't be. Remember
          -- this was the place with all the
          shells. The papier-mache shark. And you
          loved the salt water taffy.

                    LILLY
          Yeah, when I was four.

                    ELLIOT
          This is boring.

56A   EXT. THE WATER SLIDE (CLOSED FOR SEASON) - DAY   56A

Dan and the kids walk in duck/duckling formation, passing the
closed-for-the-season/very dry Water Whizz.

                    DAN
          Hang in there ...

                    ELLIOT
          This is boring.

                    BELLA
          We're bored!

                    DAN
          No, no, you're not bored. You're *boring*.

                    LILLY
          Dad!

                    DAN
          What, it's something I believe.

                    LILLY
          Yeah, but don't quote from your column.
          It's tacky.

                    DAN
          Stay with me, I have an idea. Bowling.

                                             (CONTINUED)

56A   CONTINUED: 56A

The kids immediately begin to jump up and down.

                    KIDS
          Bowling bowling bowling!

                                        HARD CUT TO:

56B   EXT. BOWLING ALLEY - DAY   56B

INSERT: Posted sign -- NEW FALL HOURS -- NOON to 10 PM.

Dan and the kids sit on the curb of the bowling alley's empty
parking lot.

                    DAN
          Life is full of disappointments. Big and
          sometimes even bigger. The key is to
          make a choice. And if it's wrong, make
          another. So what's it gonna be?
                    (beat)
          The light house or the whaling museum --
          your pick.

57   EXT. LIGHTHOUSE - DAY   57

A quintessential lighthouse on a cliff over the crashing sea.
Dan and his charge seem small standing beneath it.

                    DAN
          Do you know why we have lighthouses?

Lilly, of course, knows the answer, but she lets the littler
ones take a stab.

                    ELLIOT
          Uhm. Cause they're neat?

                    DAN
          Yes, but also, they help when it's dark
          out. To keep boats safe. To stop you
          from crashing into the rocks.
                    (gets carried away here)
          Because when you're being tossed back and
          forth by the big, dark waves, and you
          think you'll never feel land again and
          that you could split into a million
          pieces and sink to the bottom, it's the
          light that keeps you on course, it's the
          light ...

                                        (CONTINUED)

57   CONTINUED: 57

                         LILLY
                Dad? You OK?

On Dan. *Not really.* But he smiles to cover.

                         DAN
                Of course I'm OK.

58   OMITTED   58

59   OMITTED   59

60   EXT. BEACH HOUSE - DAY   60

Back home, Dan and the kids are getting out of the car when
Eileen rushes out of the house, followed by Amy.

                         EILEEN
                    (false positive)
                Hey, kids. Where you been?
                    (pointedly to Dan)
                We looked all over ...

ON DAN. *Oops.*

Still miffed, she hurries her kids inside. Amy lifts up
Bella.

                         AMY
                You know for an expert on parenting--

                         DAN
                Sorry, I wasn't thinking.

From Off, Mitch cheers -- "That's right. You go, girl!"

Turning, Dan sees Marie run out of the woods, having just
sprinted the last bit. Mitch follows soon after, ebullient.
Both of them are sweaty and out of breath.

                         MITCH
                Amazing. Dan, you shoulda seen her! She
                killed that last quarter mile.

                         MARIE
                I was -- fast -- wasn't I?

                         MITCH
                You were. It was - like I - couldn't -
                catch up.

                                              (CONTINUED)

60   CONTINUED: 60

        Beat as Mitch takes her in.

                           MITCH
                Man, even your sweat is beautiful.
                     (looking around)
                Where'd Dan go?

61   INT. BEACH HOUSE - LAUNDRY ROOM - DAY   61

        Dan falls face first into his cot. Off screen Mitch can be
        heard giving Nana a detailed account of the jog, elaborating
        particularly on Marie's many physical attributes. Dan flops
        around as Mitch goes on and on about the wonders of Marie.

                           MITCH (O.C.)
                ... she killed that last quarter mile!

                           NANA (O.C.)
                That's great -- you need some water.
                     (shouting to Marie)
                And, Marie, fresh towels - in the cabinet
                - to the right!

        Beat. Dan gets an idea.

62   OMITTED   62

63   INT. BEACH HOUSE - GIRL'S ROOM - CONTINUOUS   63

        Dan opens the door to the girl's room, Only to find ...

        Cara stretched out on the far bed by the fireplace, talking
        to Marty on her cell phone.

                           CARA
                     (softly)
                Your skin. Your smell. I miss your
                eyes.

        Dan drops to the floor and tries to sneak past, but ...

                           CARA (CONT'D)
                     (jumping up)
                Oh my God, Dad, you are such a freak!

        She rushes out, hurrying past Dan.

                                                          (CONTINUED)

                                        CARA (CONT'D)
                             (into her phone)
       No, it was my loser of a father - uh-huh,
       he was totally spying.

Cara is gone.

By way of a second entrance, Dan enters a shared bathroom and
finds ...

64   INT. BEACH HOUSE - GIRL'S BATHROOM - CONTINUOUS   64

Marie is leaning over the sink. Her face is covered with
soap and she's about to rinse off.

Dan shuts the door, startling her. He speaks quickly, they
may not have much time.

                                       MARIE
       Hello?

                                        DAN
       We gotta talk.

                                        MARIE
                         (unable to open her eyes)
       Can it (wait)...

                                        DAN
       No. Now. Is this working for you? I
       mean, really working? Be honest --

As Marie starts to rinse her face --

                                        MARIE
       I'm having a nice time.

                                          DAN
       A nice time. Really? You're enjoying
       yourself?

                                        MARIE
       I am, yes. Except for the soap in my
       eyes.

                                        DAN
       Because I'm not. And as people of
       principle, I think we need some ground
       rules. Don't you?

                                        MARIE
       Rules, OK, sure.

She reaches for the towel rack which is next to Dan.

                    DAN
          Like that! Perfect example. We need to
          keep our distance. Right now, you're too
          close. Back up. Back up!

                    MARIE
          Towel, please.

                    DAN
          Oh, right.

He hands her a towel.

                    MARIE
          Thank you.

He waits as she towel dries her face.

                    DAN
          And stop reading my book, please. Just
          stop. Also, could you not do that
          thing...

                    MARIE
          What thing?

                    DAN
          That salsa thing ...

Dan tries his best to imitate the way Marie did her salsa
move during the earlier exercise scene. Marie laughs.

                    DAN
          And if you could *not* do that - as a rule -
          that would be helpful. And I know there
          are other things that you could do, such
          as, uhm, *not exist.* That's a terrible
          thought. But for my part, as a person of
          principle, I may, from time to time, make
          myself less attractive so as to not
          encourage any inappropriate feelings on
          your part.

                    MARIE
          I'm sorry?

                    DAN
          Also, and more importantly, I will stop _
          thinking about you. Cold turkey.
                    (MORE)

                              DAN (cont'd)
                    And if I do find myself thinking about
                    you (which, in a moment of weakness, may
                    happen) I will focus all my thoughts on
                    your - uhm - flaws.

                              MARIE
                    My flaws.

                              DAN
                    Your flaws.

                              MARIE
                    And they are ...?

                              DAN
                    I have absolutely no idea, but you can be
                    certain that I'm going to find (them) --

Bathroom door swings open, Marie turns in the direction of
the door as Dan quickly steps into the bathtub/shower. Jane
enters.

                              MARIE
                    I'm in here -- !

                              JANE
                    Oh, hi, sorry. Are you taking a shower?

                              MARIE
                    No.

                              JANE
                    Do you mind if I ...?

                              MARIE
                    No. Yes! I mean, yes - I'm taking a
                    shower.

                              JANE
                    Well, then, a little advice? Old house,
                    old pipes. May I?

Before Marie can even understand Jane's request, Jane reaches
in the tub to turn on the faucet, almost touching Dan's leg.

                              JANE
                    It takes forever for the water to heat
                    up.

                              MARIE
                    Thanks.

Beat as Marie waits for Jane to leave. But she just stands
there awkwardly.

                                                       (CONTINUED)

                    JANE
            Can I talk to you about something?

                    MARIE
            Sure. Absolutely.

                    JANE
            And can we keep it between us?

Beat. Marie reaches in and pulls up the shower stop.
Water sprays down, not only drenching Dan but drowning out
the girls' conversation, which was the idea.

                    JANE
            You said this amazing thing last night.
            Actually you said a lot of amazing
            things. But what you said about, uhm,
            travel. About the importance of seeing
            the world ...

                    MARIE
            Yes?

Steam pours out the top of shower.

                    JANE
            Oh, it looks ready.

Angle on Dan, moaning as quietly as possible - the water is
exceedingly hot and all of Dan's exposed skin is turning
bright red.

Marie is about to get in the shower fully clothed.

                    JANE
            You're still dressed.

                    MARIE
            Oh, right.

                    JANE
                (turning away)
            Don't worry. I won't look.

Marie starts to undress.

                    JANE
            Well, I want to travel ...I want to go
            places ... see things I could never have
            imagined ever seeing ...

Angle on Dan in the shower. The water, still hot!

                                        (CONTINUED)

64   CONTINUED: (4)   64

Dan's POV: Through the wavy glass of the shower, the blurry
image of Marie undressing. Nice. The scalding hot water.
Not so nice.

Then the shower door slides open.

Close on Dan closing his eyes.

Marie adjusts the water temperature and, naked, steps in the
shower.

On the other side of the glass, Jane keeps talking.

                    JANE
          There's just so much of life that I want
          to - uhm - experience!

Dan can't help himself - just as he starts to squint out of
one eye, a wet washcloth lands on his face ...

65   EXT. BEACH HOUSE - MINUTES LATER   65

No, it can't be. Yes, it is. Dan, in dripping wet clothes,
climbs out the upstairs bathroom window and, in the process,
slips, then tumbles out of frame ...

66   INT. BEACH HOUSE - DAY   66

Nana finishes lunch preparations, turning away just as,
outside the window, a *blur of body* lands in a bush.

67   INT. BEACH HOUSE - KITCHEN - DAY   67

Lunchtime. Will, Rachel (who looks after Jessica), Gus,
Olivia, Bella, Lilly and Elliot are all seated at the kitchen
table. Amy is behind her daughter and Eileen is supervising.

Other Adults, including Marie, with wet hair, help carry the
food out to the dining room, where the grown-ups will be
eating.

Dan enters, his hair also wet.

                    DAN
          Mac and cheese. Nothing better.

                    POPPY
          Adults are in the dining room.

                                              (CONTINUED)

67   CONTINUED: 67

Dan and Marie make brief eye contact, but Dan can't look at
her. So he looks back at Poppy.

                    DAN
          You know what? I'm gonna mix it up and
          sit with my peeps.

Dan pulls up a chair and sits cowboy style.

                    NANA
          Danny ...

                    DAN
          Please, Mom, let me be.

68   OMITTED   68

69A   EXT. BEACH HOUSE - SHORELINE - DAY   69A

Will, Gus and Elliot skip rocks. Dan appears, watches for a
moment, then he disappears from frame. Returns. Heaves a
huge rock -- SPLASH! Then leaves.

69   INT. BEACH HOUSE - UPSTAIRS HALLWAY - DAY   69

Dan climbs the stairs to the second floor.

Dan stops outside Marie's room. Then LAUGHTER can be heard
down the hall, and Dan keeps moving...

70   INT. BEACH HOUSE - GIRL'S ROOM - DAY   70

Dan knocks (although the door is already open) and finds
Lilly and Marie gabbing away like old friends. On a table,
Lilly has spread out construction paper and other art
supplies. They're hard at work on a project.

                    DAN
          Um, hello. Hi.

                    LILLY
               (way into Marie)
          Hi.

                    DAN
               (beat, lingers)
          What are you guys up to?

(CONTINUED)

70   CONTINUED: 70

                              LILLY
                Marie's helping me with something.
                     (happily)
                We're having no fun at all.

                              DAN
                I can see that. How's she doing?

                              MARIE
                She's amazing.

                              LILLY
                Bye, Dad.

Beat as Dan leaves ... or so we think. He peeks around the
door frame. And for a moment, quietly, watches the two of
them as they resume Lilly's activity.

71   INT. BEACH HOUSE - DAY   71

Dan lying on his bed, middle of the day. Napping? If only
he could.

Nana bursts into the room. Poppy follows.

                              NANA
                I need to speak my peace. We both do.

She sits.

                              NANA
                Honey, we worry about you. You know
                that.

                              POPPY
                And what with your behavior last night
                and this morning, we are now officially
                worried.

                              NANA
                We are worried with a capital W.

                              DAN
                     (sitting up)
                Thank you, I'm touched -- but...

Howard and Amy enter, arms full with laundry.

                              DAN
                Come in...come in.

                                                    (CONTINUED)

> NANA
> We're having a private --

> HOWARD
> Oh, sorry.

> DAN
> Please stay.

> AMY
> We'll be quick …

Amy helps Howard transfer the wet clothes from the washer into the dryer.

> DAN
> Go on, Mom. I'm all ears.

Poppy closes the door.

> NANA
> You do so much for your girls and everyone else. The question is -- What are you doing for yourself?

Eileen, Rachel, and Clay appear in the doorway. Elliot is in Clay's arms. They're possibly in the middle of unloading groceries.

> CLAY
> Hey -

> POPPY
> Not now.

> NANA
> We're trying to have a private conversation.

> DAN
> No, no. Come in.

> RACHEL
> Is this about Uncle Dan acting so weird?

> NANA
> Yes.

> CLAY
> You know, I have a theory about Dan's weirdness.

                         DAN
          Oh. Oh?

                         CLAY
          Dude, you gotta be way backed up.   I
          just hope from time to time you treat
          yourself to a little self-love …

                         EILEEN
          I am so embarrassed …

                         CLAY
          No, really, my urologist says --

                         POPPY
          That's enough.

                         CARA
             (enters, leaves)
          Oh my god.

                         AMY
          The real question - the one that no one
          will ask -- "Will Dan ever find love
          again?"

                         HOWARD
          No, he won't.

                         AMY
          Howard --

                         DAN
          That's honest.

                         HOWARD
          I'm sorry. You won't. But...
             (to Dan)
          If you're open to it, maybe Love will
          find you.

                         AMY
          Awww.

Somewhere during the above lines, Mitch has appeared in the
doorway with Marie.

                         DAN
          Ah, perfect.

                         MITCH
          Hey, people --

                    CLAY
Was I clear before? Just uncork that
drain. Unclog that bottle. Am I mixing
metaphors?

                    POPPY/NANA
Yes.

                    DAN
So here's what you missed. Worried.
Love will find. Uncork the drain.

                    MITCH
Wow.

                    DAN
All right, we're done. Thank you all for
coming --

                    NANA
Actually, we're not done. We ran into
little Ruthie Draper at the Farmer's
Market.

                    POPPY
She's not so little any more.

                    NANA
She asked all about you.

                    POPPY
See, Danny, what you need is to have a
little fun.

                    NANA
Which is why she's going to pick you up
and take you for a drink.

                    DAN
Mom. Come on. No.

                    MITCH
          (horrified)
Ruthie Draper?

                    NANA
What?
          (losing her patience)
What is it, Mitch? Just say it!

                    MITCH
Ruthie 'Pig Face' Draper? Mom, Dad, what
are you thinking?

                                        (CONTINUED)

                              POPPY
                    That's enough, Mitchell.

                              CLAY
                    No, Pops, I agree. Not Pigface Draper.
                    That's downright cruel.

Someone snorts. Most everyone -- even Amy -- laughs.

                              NANA
                    You're going. It's already decided.

                              POPPY
                    You'll have a good time.

                              DAN
                    No, no. I don't even remember Ruthie
                    Draper. I don't want to go. I don't
                    want to go with the Pigface.

                              MITCH
                    We'll go double. It'll be fun. Right,
                    Marie?

                              MARIE
                    Yes.
                         (beat)
                    It'll be fun.

Beat. She snorts. The group (sans Dan) laughs.

71A   INT. FAMILY ROOM - BEACH HOUSE - NIGHT   71A

Dan stands near the fireplace, dreading what is to come. He
has changed his clothes something akin to a kid being forced
to dress up for church. He is not at ease in himself.

Clay and Mitch are at the piano performing "Pig Face Draper."
Everyone sings.

Others have casually positioned themselves around the room,
including Jane. Dan looks to her and kind of shrugs.

                              JANE
                    Dad, it's no fun to have a dad who has no
                    fun.

Permission granted.

From off, we hear a bell. Nana moves off to the door.

Marie watches what is going on, and finds it amusing.

                                                    (CONTINUED)

> NANA (O.S.)
> Come in, come in!

> RUTHIE DRAPER (O.S.)
> Your house, it's just the way I remember
> it!

Nana leads Ruthie into the room.

Dan can't believe it. Neither can Mitch.

Guess who enters the house and makes heads turn? A beauty.
Flame red hair. The ugly duckling is all grown up.

Marie crosses her arms and looks -- dare we say -- a wee bit
threatened.

> RUTHIE
> Hello, Dan. I'd know you anywhere. You
> look just the same.

> DAN
> Ruthie, you look ... great.

72   INT. BAR - NIGHT   72

The Two 'Couples' sit at a table. Dan sits next to Ruthie.
Marie sits next to Mitch.

The other patrons are 'locals.' The music from the CD jute
box blares.

> MARIE
> How do you two know each other?

> RUTHIE
> He was my first.

On Dan. *What?*

> RUTHIE (CONT'D)
> Baby-sitter.

> DAN
> Oh. Oh, right.

> MITCH
> Remember the diaper incident?

> DAN
>   (to Marie)
> It's a story we don't tell much.

(CONTINUED)

                         MITCH
          Try to spare Dan the profound
          embarrassment ...

                         DAN
          So let's not tell it now.

                         MARIE
          What's the diaper incident?

                         RUTHIE
          Apparently he'd never changed a diaper
          before and when he got mine off he kind
          of panicked -- And you called 911.

                         DAN
          Did not.

                         RUTHIE
          Yes, you did.

A burst of laughter all around.

                         MITCH
          Harvard Medical School. John Hopkins.
          You've certainly done well for yourself,
          Ruthie.

                         DAN
          Yes. It's impressive.

                         MITCH
              (angling)
          I can't imagine you had much time for
          dating.

                         RUTHIE
          That couldn't be more true. Although
          there was someone ... someone very
          special in my life ... but he was ...
              (suddenly emotional)
          Lost in a freak accident ...
              (tearing up)
          I'm sorry.

Mitch offers a cocktail napkin.

                         RUTHIE
          Thank you. What's weird is that we'd
          only known each other for three days.
          But you know how sometimes you just know.

                                          (CONTINUED)

                    MARIE
Yes.

Mitch, while staring at Ruthie, takes one of Marie's hands
and gives it a squeeze.

                    MITCH
Absolutely, yes. So you're a doctor?

                    RUTHIE
Yes.

                    MARIE
And what's your specialty?

                    RUTHIE
I'm a plastic surgeon.

                    MARIE
Of course you are.

                    RUTHIE
I work exclusively with burn victims and
children born with facial deformities.

                    MITCH
             (enthusiastically to Dan)
So basically she's a saint.

                    RUTHIE
I'd like to think I'm doing my little bit
to help. Like your brother.

                    DAN
Stop.

                    RUTHIE
Confession. Sometimes when I can't
sleep, I go on-line and read your past
columns.
             (to Marie)
Have you read Dan?

                    MARIE
Only his fiction.

                    RUTHIE
You're in for a treat.
             (to Dan)
What you said to Marlene in Montclair
whose son was 15. "Stop the madness.
He's got to make his own bed!"
Brilliant.
             (MORE)

> RUTHIE (cont'd)
> And to "Mother of a Couch Potato - Hide
> the remote. So what if he has to get up
> to change the channel, at least it's
> exercise!" Brilliant. Oh, oh and this
> one - "To the Parents of Five Picky
> Eaters who made individualized meals for
> each kid - What are you, a restaurant?"

> MARIE
> Brilliant.

> MITCH
> She remembers your every word.

> RUTHIE
> I have a photographic memory.

> MITCH
> And the brains of Einstein.

> RUTHIE
> All I'm saying is -- I don't have kids
> and I don't have problems, but it's clear
> that if one day I do, your words will
> bring me comfort.

For Marie, there's so much ass-kissing going on, you can
almost hear the SMOOCH of lips.

Dan notices that Marie suddenly has a bit of an edge, and
that Ruthie is the cause. *Hmmm, interesting.*

Mitch, on the other hand, becomes more convinced that this
Ruthie is the girl for Dan.

The music playing under the scene begins to work its way up
the spine of Ruthie Draper. Pent up, she starts a dance of
sorts in her chair, much to Marie's dismay. Dan appears
impervious, although it does infect Mitch who might begin to
drum on the table or bob his head.

> RUTHIE (CONT'D)
> I'm sorry, I can't help myself. If
> you'll excuse me ...

Unable to stand it any longer, Ruthie shoots to her feet and
moves to the jukebox and begins a comely dance of her own
devising.

> MITCH
> I'm sorry, dude, but the way she's moving
> can only make a guy wonder.

Dan clears his throat, indicates Marie.

                    MITCH (CONT'D)
          No, Marie's cool. You're cool, right?

Marie is at a loss.

                    MARIE
          Sure, I'm cool. But I don't think Dan is
          interested in (her) ...

                    MITCH
          You're not?

                    DAN
          I'm not?

                    MARIE
          I don't think you are. Are you?

Apparently he is, because as the music changes, Dan stands,
strides to the center of the dance area, points to Ruthie,
who is pleasantly surprised to see him standing there. With
one finger, he gestures for her to come in his direction.
She does as he says, joining in the middle of the club, and
they dance, oh boy do they ever.

As Mitch calls out, 'Yes, yes!' Dan and Ruthie tear up the
dance floor.

                    MITCH
          I don't know what it was, but something
          was holding him back.

                    MARIE
          Not anymore.

Angle on Dan who is a wild man on the dance floor. Ruthie is
doing her best to keep up.

                    MITCH
          And that's a beautiful thing.

For Mitch, maybe. But maybe not for Marie who suddenly grabs
Mitch by the hand and pulls him onto the dance floor. There,
a dancing duel of sorts plays out with an ever-increasing
intensity of moves, culminating with Dan letting loose in a
near orgasmic frenzy. Our other three stop and watch.

73   EXT. BEACH HOUSE - INSIDE RUTHIE'S CAR - NIGHT   73

Ruthie's sports car skids to a stop. Dan is in the passenger
seat.

                                (CONTINUED)

73   CONTINUED: 73

Marie and Mitch are squeezed in the back. As they all climb
out:

                         MITCH
               I really love your car.

                         MARIE
               OK, nice meeting you, Ruth! Come on,
               guys!

                         RUTHIE
               Actually ...

Marie turns.

                         RUTHIE (CONT'D)
               Dan and I are going for a drive.

Marie looks at Dan. *Is that true?*

                         DAN
                    (beat)
               And don't wait up.

Ruthie gets back in the car.

In the background - Mitch celebrates.

Dan gets in and gives Marie a subtle but cruel look as he and
Ruthie drive off.

And Marie watches the car go.

                                        SCREEN TO BLACK:

74   INT. BEACH HOUSE - KITCHEN - DAY   74

Next morning. The breakfast table. Attendance is at
capacity. Why? Marie is making her famous pancakes.

Dan enters and takes his place at the table.

                         MITCH
               Better and better with every bite.

                         HOWARD
               Words cannot describe.

                         DAN
               How are they, Lil'?

                                              (CONTINUED)

> LILLY
> Oh, Dad, they're scrumptious.

> POPPY
> Truly mouth watering!

> GUS
> I'm on my third stack.

> HOWARD
> And there's no stopping him. Is there
> Gus?

Gus shakes his head, "No."

Dan looks around. Big, fluffy, menu-worthy pancakes have
been served piping hot to the others. Everyone is eating --
it's a kind of breakfast heaven.

> LILLY
> (to Dan)
> More please. It's a secret recipe, but
> she let me crack the eggs.

It's almost eerie, and certainly impressive -- the way
everyone is eating, making soft groans of approval as they
chew -- never have pancakes made such an impact.

Most of those eating are finished and syrup-coated plates are
carried to the sink. Those with happy stomachs call out:
"Those were great" "Best ever" "Not only do I thank you but
my stomach thanks you."

On Marie, basking.

Everyone else exits leaving Dan, Mitch and Clay (who holds
baby Jessica) alone with Marie.

> CLAY
> So how's Mr. Lucky this morning?

> DAN
> It was fun.

Bang as Marie slams the skillet down.

> CLAY
> I bet you worked up an appetite last
> night.

> DAN
> Actually I am kind of ... hungry ...

(CONTINUED)

74   CONTINUED: (2)   74

                              CLAY
                  Did you uncork? Have you unclogged?

                              MITCH
                  Whatever happened, no one deserves
                  someone more than you.

Only Dan notices Marie's erratic behavior. And part of him
is enjoying the show, at least until ...

Marie serves Dan his much-anticipated stack of pancakes. Dan
looks down. *What?* They're burnt black.

Dan looks up just as his nephew, Will Burns, enters the room,
tossing a football to his dad.

                              POPPY
                  Not at the table. Take it outside!

Everyone files out, leaving Dan alone with Marie. He stares
at her -- and she stares back -- as he brings a burnt pancake
to his mouth and takes a bite. Crunch.

75   EXT. BEACH HOUSE - THE BACK YARD - DAY   75

It is spirited game of touch football and most everyone is
playing. Most notably, though, Dan and Marie are on opposing
teams.

Mitch heaves the football ...

Dan prepares to catch the pass ...

The football in mid-flight ...

Dan stretches out his arms -- the ball touches his hands,
then ...

Wham. He's tackled. Sprawled on the ground, he looks back
and sees Marie was the cause. She brushes herself off and
hurries back to the huddle.

Nana and Poppy watch from the porch. Lilly is on the steps
with Elliot and Bella.

A later play -- Marie has the ball. She's fast. She pivots,
she spins, she dodges opponents ...

Dan comes up from the secondary -- and instead of tagging, he
leaps on top of her. At the last moment, Marie laterals the
ball to Cara who catches it and with Clay blocking, runs for
a touchdown.

                                                    (CONTINUED)

Few notice that Dan has ended up on top of Marie. But Lilly
does.

For a moment they look at each other. An intimate moment.

Then Marie rolls him over and pins him down.

She gets up and runs back to the huddle.

Dan props up on his elbows, watches her go, fighting a smile,
thinking *Oh yeah!*

                         MITCH
               Look out for the --!

Then *SMACK!* The football hits Dan in the face. More to the
point, the nose. Dan covers his face in pain.

76   EXT. BEACH HOUSE - PORCH - DAY   76

Dan sits, his head tilted back, a wad of Kleenex up one
nostril. Nana serves as Nurse as the football game continues
in the yard.

                         NANA
               Why you persist in acting like a fifteen-
               year-old is beyond me.

                         DAN
                    (joking, but not)
               I'm filled with reckless desire.

Poppy brings tissues and ice.

                         NANA
               You need to be filled with greater
               restraint.

Dan's cell phone rings.

                         DAN
               What does that mean?

                         NANA
               I think you know what that means.

                         DAN
                    (pulling his phone out of his
                     pocket and handing it to
                     Poppy)
               Dad, could you --

                                                    (CONTINUED)

> POPPY
> Hello. No, I'm his dad.
> (handing Dan the phone)
> Someone named Jordy. For you.

77   EXT. BEACH HOUSE - PORCH AND YARD - A MOMENT LATER   77

The football game is still in progress. Nana rings a bell.

Everyone turns.

Nana and Poppy stand at the top of the porch steps.

> NANA
> Big news, everybody! Dan just got a
> phone call --

> POPPY
> And keep in mind that syndication is
> everything when you're a columnist --

> NANA
> He's going to be read all over.

> DAN
> Mom, Dad, please -- I can explain it.

Dan steps between them.

> DAN (CONT'D)
> I've been asked to meet with upper
> management of the Lamson Newspaper Group.
> They're driving here tomorrow ... to sit
> down ... with me ...

The group cheers.

Poppy, on the other hand, says:

> POPPY
> Maybe you should get the job first, son.

ON DAN as the family members begin to disperse.

Jane lingers. Dan sits down next to her. Will and Elliot
run up the stairs.

> JANE
> Dad, Lilly just asked me why you were
> flirting with Marie during the football
> game.
> (beat)
> (MORE)

77 CONTINUED: 77

> JANE (cont'd)
> Don't worry, I covered for you. I told
> her it was nothing.

> DAN
> Because it was.

> JANE
> Dad, I'm seventeen, okay? You were SO
> flirting.

Beat. Busted.

> JANE (CONT'D)
> It doesn't matter anyway. It's not like
> she's the least bit interested in you.
> But cool it, OK? Congratulations.

Jane goes, leaving Dan alone on the porch.

SCENES 78-82 OMITTED.

83   EXT. BEACH HOUSE - DOOR TO STORAGE AREA UNDER PORCH - DAY   83

Dan looks back for help with the jackets. But Will and Gus
are gone. Hmmm. He looks out and sees ...

84   EXT. BEACH HOUSE - BACKYARD - DAY   84

In the corner of the yard, Elliot, Will and Gus peer down on
the rocks. Something has captured their attention. Dan
walks toward them.

85   EXT. ROCKS ON THE SHORE - MOMENTS LATER   85

Angle on Elliot, Will and Gus peering down. Dan's face comes
into frame, wanting to see what all the fuss is about.

DAN'S POV: Cara on the rocks, Cara kissing a boy, the boy is
Marty Barasco ...

On Cara looking up at her dad.

> CARA
> Oh shit.

86   INT. BEACH HOUSE - MOMENTS LATER   86

The boys run SCREAMING toward the house ...

86   CONTINUED: 86

Nana and Others look out the window.

Marie looks up from her book.

Marie's POV: Dan leads Cara by the arm toward the house.
Marty follows. As they get close to the door, Amy, Eileen,
and the Kids scatter.

                         CARA
               He has relatives in Boston!

Cara runs into the house.

                         DAN
                    (turning back to Marty)
               You, stay there.

Dan follows Cara. Marty slips onto the porch.

                         CARA
               Dad, he missed me so much that he took a
               bus--

87   INT. BEACH HOUSE - STUDY - LATER THAT DAY   87

Dan closes the two pocket doors, in effect giving him privacy
with Cara.

                         DAN
               What was going on out there?

                         CARA
               You don't have to worry -- when it comes
               to sex, Marty is the one who wants to
               wait.

                         DAN
               What about that sentence is supposed to
               bring me comfort?

                         CARA
               Dad. I love him. I love him I love him
               I love him.

88   INT. BEACH HOUSE - FAMILY ROOM - CONTINUOUS   88

Marie, in the next room, smiles. She and Other Family
Members can't help but listen as the *walls are so thin.*

88   CONTINUED: 88

(Throughout the rest of the scene, shots of other family
members listening will be intercut. The last shot will be of
Marie.)

                    DAN (O.S.)
          No. You don't.

                    CARA (O.S.)
          What we have is true love, and just
          because you don't have it ...

89   INT. BEACH HOUSE - STUDY - CONTINUOUS   89

                    CARA
          Doesn't mean you should punish us --

                    DAN
          Infatuation is not love. Sexual
          attraction is not love --

                    CARA
          You don't understand.

                    DAN
          I don't understand?

                    CARA
          No, you don't. You don't even understand
          that you don't understand.

                    DAN
          What, that it's -- it's frustrating that
          you can't be with this person -- that
          there's something keeping you apart --
          that there's something about this person
          that you really connect with and that
          being near this person makes you sweat
          and dizzy and you know if you could just
          be together-- that this person would help
          you become the best possible version of
          yourself, and --

On Cara, as it dawns - *Ohmigod. He understands.*

On Dan. *What did I just say?*

                    CARA
          So Marty can stay?

90   EXT. BEACH HOUSE - DAY   90

Apparently not. It's Good-bye to Marty time. Dan leads
Marty out of the house to Howard's car which is idling right
out front.

>   MARTY
>   Mr. Burns, I would never do anything --

>   DAN
>   I'm sure. But Howard is going to drive
>   you to the bus. We called your aunt.
>   She'll be waiting for you in Boston.

>   MARTY
>   Yes, sir.

Dan opens the car door. Marty gets in the back seat.

>   DAN
>   (quietly)
>   Look, I'm not your parent -- but I think
>   you should know: Love is a dangerous
>   feeling.

>   MARTY
>   No, sir …

>   DAN
>   Are you arguing with me?

>   MARTY
>   No. I'm just saying. El amor no es un
>   sentimiento. Es una habilidad.

Beat. Dan doesn't understand.

>   MARTY
>   (translating)
>   "Love is not a feeling. It's an
>   ability."

>   DAN
>   Who told you that?

>   MARTY
>   I made it up myself, Mr. Burns.

Beat. *This is some kid.* Dan closes the car door.

Dan turns back to Cara on the porch. She is surrounded by a
few allies -- Jane, Marie and Nana.

                                            (CONTINUED)

                    DAN
          Come say good-bye.

Cara approaches Marty and just as they're about to touch,
Cara blurts out --

                    CARA
          I miss you already.

                    DAN (CONT'D)
          Window. Okay, that's it!

The electric window closes.

                    JANE
          Dad.

                    DAN
          She'll see him soon enough.

Dan signals for Howard to drive away. But the moment the car
takes off, Cara makes a desperate sprint and chases after the
car. Jane follows.

On the steps outside the house, Marie moves next to Dan.

                    MARIE
          That's sweet.

                    DAN
          What's sweet? How is that sweet?

                    MARIE
          To be that certain ... to feel so much
          love ...

                    DAN
          Pshaw. Love isn't a feeling ...

                    MARIE
          No?

                    DAN
          It's an ability.

With the car out-of-view, Cara falls to the ground, sobbing.
It's Greek, her grief. Jane runs to comfort her.

                    MARIE
          Well, if that's true you have one gifted
          daughter.

(CONTINUED)

STILLS

Alison Pill as Jane.

Brittany Robertson
as Cara.

Marlene Lawston as Lilly.

Steve Carell as Dan Burns.

Juliette Binoche as Marie.

Dan meets Marie.

Steve Carell, Juliette Binoche, and Dane Cook as Mitch.

Aerobics on the lawn.

Dan watches Marie and Mitch
stretch as Lilly looks on.

Dan takes Lilly, Bella (Willa Cuthrell-Tuttleman), and Elliot (CJ Adams) on an outing.

Clay (Norbert Leo Butz), Mitch, Rachel (Ella Miller), and Cara during the Ruthie "Pigface" sing-a-long.

Emily Blunt as Ruthie Draper.

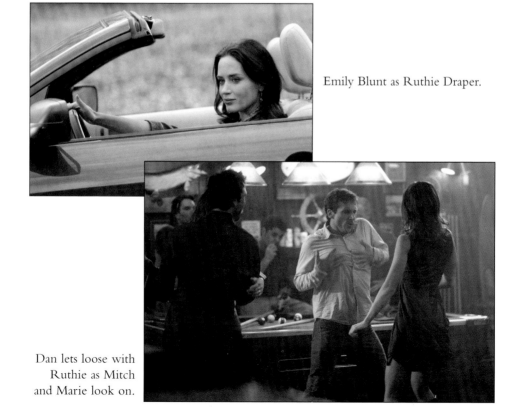

Dan lets loose with Ruthie as Mitch and Marie look on.

First Assistant Director Steve Dunn, a wet Steve Carell, and Writer/Director Peter Hedges watch the video playback.

John Mahoney as Poppy and
Dianne Wiest as Nana.

Producers Brad Epstein and Jon Shestack.

Writer Pierce Gardner.

Lawrence Sher, Steve Dunn, Peter Hedges, and Production Designer Sarah Knowles.

Costume Designer Alix Friedberg and Executive Producer Mari Jo Winkler-Ioffreda.

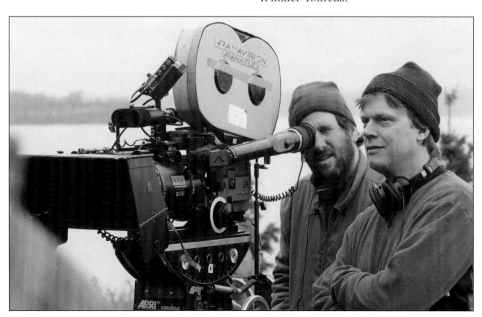

Lawrence Sher and Peter Hedges.

Steve Carell, Juliette Binoche, and Peter Hedges in between takes.

Lawrence Sher, Peter Hedges, Co-Producer/Script Supervisor Dianne Dreyer, and Sarah Knowles with Brad Epstein and Jon Shestack in the background.

90   CONTINUED: (2)   90

                         CARA
                   (in the distance now, turns and
                    screams)
                You are a Murderer of Love!!!

91   INT. BEACH HOUSE - LIVING ROOM - LATER THAT DAY   91

Cara -- with her mascara tear-stained face -- hasn't
completely recovered but she helps Jane take down names and
talents. Amy and Eileen are hanging decorations.

                         AMY
                Olivia has something with the girls. Gus
                will be doing his usual. Bella is on the
                fence. Howard and I will sing.

                         JANE
                   (as she writes)
                That's nice. Aunt Eileen?

Eileen is about to answer when Dan passes by.

                         DAN
                Put me down.

                         EILEEN
                Really? What's your talent?

                         DAN
                   (as he goes)
                Murderer of love.

                         JANE
                You were saying?

                         EILEEN (O.S.)
                We have something planned with the whole
                family.

92   INT. BEACH HOUSE - LIVING ROOM - NIGHT   92

Furniture has been moved to create an audience area which
faces a make-shift stage. The performance area is lit with
Chinese lanterns. The whole setting has been 'thrown
together' on the cheap but with great love.

Jane, the MC for this year's festivities, steps forward.
She holds a clipboard.

                                                      (CONTINUED)

                    JANE
          First up, our circus family: Cirque Du
          Sol Clay.

The family is seated throughout the room. Nana and Poppy
share the biggest, cushiest chair. Kids sit on laps, on the
floor. They clap and cheer for Jane.

Angle on Dan sitting off in the far corner, curiously removed
from the festivities.

As Clay and his family do a circus act.

                    MARIE
               (to Cara, who is next to her)
          What's your dad's talent?

                    CARA
          Doesn't have one.

                    LILLY
          He's the only one excused from
          participating ...

Meanwhile, a nervous Mitch sidles up to Dan.

                    MITCH
          Hey, bro. I don't have a good feeling.

                    DAN
          It'll be fine. Just do what you always
          do.

                    MITCH
          No, Marie's not a lip sync type of girl.
          I gotta do something special.

                    DAN
          Just be yourself.

Bella and her imitation of barking dogs, followed by Cara,
who stands before the group, eyes still puffy from crying.

                    CARA
          This is for Marty.

She holds up a cherry. She bites off the stem, discards the
cherry and attempts to tie it into a knot with her tongue.

                                              (CONTINUED)

                        DAN
                 (under his breath)
    Oh.

Other, various reaction shots.

Finally, she takes the knotted stem and holds it up as if to say "Tada!".

The room erupts in applause.

MUSIC/SCORE

Quick shots of various acts.

Lilly, Olivia, and Rachel do a routine with plastic cups.

Nana and Poppy do an act of their own which involves mental telepathy and physical transfer.

Amy and Howard sing a duet from *Don Giovanni*.

During their duet, Mitch walks over to Dan.

                      MITCH
    I have an idea.

                      DAN
    I'm sure it'll be great.

                      MITCH
               (holds up a guitar)
    It could be.

                                        CUT TO:

CLOSE ON JANE:

                      JANE
    And last ... but certainly not least ...
    Uncle Mitch.

Mitch appears before the crowd. He smiles and says:

                      MITCH
    Someone very wise -- my brother -- once
    said -- "If you want to be completely
    honest -- sing."

                    EILEEN
    Oh please, no.

                    MITCH
     But first, I'd like to introduce my band.

Mitch points to Dan who is already seated, tuning a guitar.
He has positioned himself so he's practically sitting with
his back to the audience. His intention is only to accompany
Mitch.

                    AMY
     I don't believe it.

Marie, turning as if to say "Believe what?"

                    AMY (CONT'D)
     He hasn't played since she –

                    MITCH
     Needless to say, this song is dedicated
     to ... a certain someone.

                    MITCH (CONT'D)
          (under his breath)
     So here goes nothing.

Mitch is very nervous.

                    DAN
          (whispers)
     Mitch. Trust the song.

Mitch nods that he's ready and Dan plays the first chords of
the Pete Townshend's <u>LET MY LOVE OPEN THE DOOR</u>.

                    MITCH
          (barely audible)
     When people keep repeating
     That you'll never fall in love
     When everybody keeps retreating
     But you can't seem to get enough
     Let my love open the door
     Let my love open the door
     Let my love open the door
     To your heart

Dan strums the chord, waiting for Mitch, who has gone blank.
Mitch looks to Dan for help.

                    DAN/MITCH
     When everything feels all over
     When everybody seems unkind
     I'll give you a four-leaf clover
     Take all the worry out of your mind
     Let my love open the door
          (MORE)

>   DAN/MITCH (cont'd)
>   *Let my love open the door*
>   *Let my love open the door*

For a few bars, Mitch does his best to sing with Dan. But
Mitch's mouth is drying out, his tongue can't seem to work
right, he lacks breath support. For Mitch, all systems are
down. And while Dan's voice is not the greatest, it's not
bad either - sincere and, at least, audible.

>   DAN
>   *I have the only key to your heart*
>   *I can stop you falling apart*
>   *Release yourself from misery*
>   *Only one thing's gonna set you free*
>   *That' my love*

>   DAN/MITCH
>   *Let my love open the door*
>   *Let my love open the door*
>   *Let my love open the door*
>   *To your heart*

Somewhere around here Mitch drops out and it's only Dan
singing now.

>   DAN (CONT'D)
>   *When tragedy befalls you*
>   *Don't let them bring you down*
>   *Love can cure your problem*
>   *You're so lucky I'm around*

The once raucous room is now very subdued - everyone
listening as Dan sings for the first time in years.

>   DAN (CONT'D)
>   *Let my love open the door*
>   *Let my love open the door*
>   *Let my love open the door*
>   *To your heart*

Angle on Marie, barely able to breathe. Dan finishes playing
to a pin-drop silent room.

More people are wiping eyes than clapping. Mitch takes a
bow. Then he points to Dan and, over the applause, shouts to
Marie:

>   MITCH
>   What he said!

Marie does her best to smile. *Something has shifted.*

93   INT. BEACH HOUSE - LAUNDRY ROOM/DAN'S ROOM - NIGHT   93

Dan is changing into his sleep clothes -- a T-shirt and
flannel pajama pants.

The door to the laundry starts to open. Marie slips in,
she's angry and upset.

                    DAN
          Mom, please knock -- oh, hello.

                    MARIE
          So what was that? What were you
          thinking?

                    DAN
          He wanted my help.

                    MARIE
          That's you being helpful?

                    DAN
          I know -- I couldn't stop myself.
              (Beat)
          Look, it took a lot for him to sing for
          you --

                    MARIE
          You sang for me. We have a serious
          problem.

Dan looks at Marie.

                    DAN
          What do you mean?

                    MITCH (O.S.)
          Marie?

Marie tosses his book on the bed.

                    MARIE
          Page 192. "Did I just die? Because
          an angel walked into the room."

                    DAN
          It's an honest mistake.

                    MARIE
          Page 248 -- "I forgive you your
          past, if you forgive me mine." It
          seems all his best lines were yours.

                                        (CONTINUED)

                         DAN
          But he's-

                         MARIE
          And what makes it worse is that you're
          such a good guy, you weren't even going
          to take the credit.

                         MITCH (O.C.)
          Anybody seen Marie?

                         MARIE
             (calling out)
          Coming.
             (to Dan)
          I don't know if I can keep pretending.

                         DAN
             (terrified)
          You can.
             (beat)
          We have to.

Marie leaves. Dan sits. His head in his hands.

                         LILLY (O.C.)
          Dad?

                         DAN
          Yeah, peanut.

                         LILLY (O.C.)
          Can you come up to my room? There's
          something I want to show you.

                         DAN
          Can we do it tomorrow? I promise.

                         LILLY (O.C.)
          Sure thing, Dad.

Dan reaches up and turns out the light.

94   INT. BEACH HOUSE - LAUNDRY ROOM/DAN'S ROOM - MORNING   94

Dan sleeps. He stirs, instinctively reaching out his arm for
the person next to him. *But no one is there.*

Dan opens his eyes. *Gotta stop doing that.*

95   OMITTED   95

96   INT. BEACH HOUSE - KITCHEN - DAY   96

                         EILEEN/CLAY
               Shhh.

He enters the kitchen and sees that family members are
peeking out of every available window.

Dan squeezes in to see for himself ...

Dan's POV through window: Marie and Mitch in the driveway.
From the looks of things, Marie is breaking up with Mitch.
They hug goodbye.

Angle from outside:

Every window in the house has at least one family member
looking out.

Marie gets in the car and drives away.

Mitch watches.

Standing near Dan, Eileen lets out a phew ...

Which turns out to be premature because a composed Mitch
starts kicking a pile of raked leaves.

97   INT. BEACH HOUSE - KITCHEN - DAY   97

Mitch enters. The Post Mortem. Amy, Clay, Eileen, Nana and
Dan are gathered around Mitch. Jane, Poppy and Howard are
also there. Everyone is trying to console Mitch.

                    MITCH
               She said I'm a great guy. She said she
               loved me a lot...but that we should both
               probably find our true soulmates.

                    AMY
                    (interrupting)
               OK, now that she's gone, I can say it.
               I've had my suspicions about her. She
               was too nice and smart and pretty and...
               nice.

                    EILEEN
               And the way she joined in all the family
               activities ... it was ... and the way she
               played with the kids was ... was ...

                                              (CONTINUED)

97   CONTINUED: 97

                    MITCH
          Yes?

                    EILEEN
          Actually she was really good with the
          kids.

                    CLAY
          But there was one time I thought she was
          totally rude --

                    AMY
          When?

                    CLAY
          Turned out I was wrong -- but I could
          see, if pushed, how she could be.

                    MITCH
               (staring in Dan's direction)
          There has to be something. Some reason
          she ...

                    DAN
               (defensively)
          Why are you looking at me?

                    MITCH
          I'm not looking at you.

                    HOWARD
          He's just looking into the vast void that
          is his future. You just happen to be
          there.

                    AMY
          Danny, do you have anything to add?

                    CLAY
          Yeah, what does the expert have to say?
          Help us out here.

This snaps Mitch out of his funk. He turns to Dan, who
doesn't know what to say. Fortunately, for Dan, Nana blurts
out ...

                    NANA
          The hard fact is...we all liked her a
          lot...

                    JANE
          Yeah, we really did.

                                              (CONTINUED)

97   CONTINUED: (2)   97

        Mitch looks around, sees the population of the room has
        doubled.

                        MITCH
                This isn't helping. Somebody please
                think of something fun to do!

98   OMITTED   98

99   INT. BEACH HOUSE - FAMILY ROOM - DAY   99

        Everyone, including Dan, plays a quickly thrown-together game
        of Celebrity. Two teams. Fierce competition. Eileen is
        giving the clues. Answers include: "Sammy Davis Jr."
        "Georgia O'Keeffe." "Helen Keller." Mitch takes over. His
        clue: A gift from France.

        Dan's phone vibrates.

                        DAN
                Jordy, hey!

                        GROUP
                The Statue of Liberty.

                        MARIE (ON FILTER)
                You can't talk.

                        MITCH
                He put the key on the kite. Glasses.
                Electricity.

                        DAN
                No, but go on ... Ben Franklin.

        At the same time, Mitch gives out the next clues:

                        MITCH
                Okay -- she's got beautiful eyes ...

                        MARIE (ON FILTER)
                I had to leave ...

                        DAN
                Yes ... I know.

                        MITCH
                Sweet smile.

                        MARIE (ON FILTER)
                But the truth is:

                                                        (CONTINUED)

                              MITCH
                    A one of a kind woman.

                              DAN
                    Yes...

                              MARIE (ON FILTER)
                    I didn't get very far.

                              SOMEONE IN THE GROUP
                    Marie!

Mitch falls to his knees and then drops his head into the
bowl of clues.

And with that this particular game of Celebrity comes to a
crashing halt. Except for Dan, who, in response to Marie's
news, says ...

                              DAN
                    Yes.

100   EXT. BEACH HOUSE - DAY   100

Dan sneaks to his car, only to be stopped by ...

Lilly who stands in the yard.

                              LILLY
                    Dad?

                              DAN
                         (turns back)
                    Hey, you.

                              LILLY
                    Can I show you what I made?

                              DAN
                    First thing, when I get back, OK?

Dan heads to the car.

                              LILLY (O.S.)
                    Okay.

101   EXT. OCEAN DRIVE ROAD - DAY   101

Dan races in his car down Ocean Drive Road. It hugs the
coastline.

101   CONTINUED: 101

The road is empty and, without realizing it, he shoots past a
stop sign.

That's when the SHRILL WAIL of a Police Siren can be heard.
And a Police Car speeds after Dan, in hot pursuit.

102   EXT. SIDE OF ROAD - DAY   102

Dan has pulled over. The Policeman approaches and, sure
enough, he's the same Rhode Island cop from before.

                    POLICEMAN
          You again.

                    DAN
               (unusually chipper)
          Nice to see you, officer. How are you
          today?

                    POLICEMAN
          Do you know why I pulled you over?

                    DAN
          I sure do. I know what I was doing. And
          I know it's all wrong.

Beat. Policeman looks at him curiously. *This is some
strange bird.*

                    POLICEMAN
          This is gonna cost you.

                    DAN
          Put it on my tab.

                    POLICEMAN
          What was that?

                    DAN
               (laughs)
          Put it on my tab.

103   EXT. A STREET DOWNTOWN - DAY   103

Angle from inside Dan's car -- the windshield wipers sweep
the rain away as Dan drives through ... looking for ...
looking for ...

104   EXT. BOWLING ALLEY - DAY   104

Marie's car which is parked outside a bowling alley. She
waits in her car.

Dan pulls up next to her. He gets out of his car and climbs
into hers.

They look at each other, searching for what to say. Rain
continues to fall. Behind them, a large neon outline of a
bowling pin *blinks.*

Marie, the braver of the two, finally says:

                    MARIE
          What are we doing?

                    DAN
          Uhm. It may be wrong ...

                    MARIE
          Yes ...

                    DAN
          But there's a certain rightness to our
          wrongness, I think ...

                    MARIE
          I think we've got to think. I mean, your
          girls. And how do we ... I mean, they're
          extraordinary. And, what?

                    DAN
               (enjoying her)
          I think this is all premature.

                    MARIE
          You do?

                    DAN
          We don't even know if you can bowl.

105   OMITTED   105

106   INT. BOWLING ALLEY - MOMENTS LATER   106

Marie goes first. She positions her sparkly bowling ball
expertly. Brings the ball back -- her form is exquisite --
the ball speeds down the lane ...

                                              (CONTINUED)

106   CONTINUED: 106

Into the gutter.

Dan laughs.

Instead of waiting for her ball to return, Marie takes Dan's ball, lets it roll and all ten pins scatter. Strike!

Quick shots as they bowl the first few frames. They are having a BLAST.

The only other bowlers in the alley are an OLD COUPLE. They can't help but notice the two 'teenagers' in Lane 7.

The BOWLING ALLEY MANAGER notices as well. At the perfect moment, he reaches over, hits a switch. And the lights change.

The effect is psychedelic, magical, intimate. It's now virtually impossible to see anything beyond Dan and Marie's immediate lane. The alleys and pins glow.

Dan looks at Marie. The image of her face, rainbowed by a mirror ball which spins above, mesmerizes him.

Finally, Dan throws a ball which appears to be a strike. 9 pins fall. One wobbles ...

Dan is crouched down, waving for the pin to fall.

Marie is behind him, praying for the same result.

                    DAN (CONT'D)
          Come on, come on ...

Dan and Marie celebrate. And then they kiss.

It's quite a kiss for a first kiss. In fact, they're so deep into their kiss that they don't notice as the regular lights turn on.

                    LILLY (O.S.)
          Dad?

Dan stops. He and Marie turn.

Standing there -- the Burns Family. All of them.

                    JANE
          Oh my God, Dad, what are you doing?

                    MITCH
          Marie? What the hell is going on?

                                              (CONTINUED)

Dan laughs nervously. Then ...

                    DAN
          Look, I can explain -- You guys broke
          up, right? Am I right?

                    MITCH
          Two hours ago. We broke up two hours
          ago!

                    POPPY
          Son, what is going on?

                    MITCH
               (to Marie)
          I thought you left!

                    DAN
          She *did* leave. She just didn't get very
          far.

                    JANE
          What?

                    DAN
          Let me explain it.

                    MITCH
          Yeah. Let him explain it.

Everyone grows silent. Dan looks at the circle of shocked
faces around him. He gathers his courage.

                    DAN
          Remember the woman in the book store?
          Here she is. You told me to go after her
          - and I didn't.

                    MARIE
          It wasn't planned.

                    DAN
          I know how it looks. But I also know how
          it feels. How this feels.

                    MITCH
               (punching him)
          See how this feels, you sonofabitch --

Dan is knocked to the ground. Mitch stands over him.

                                              (CONTINUED)

106   CONTINUED: (3)   106

                              MARIE
                      (to Nana and Poppy)
                 I'm sorry. I'm so, so sorry.

In tears, Marie flees the bowling alley ...

Dan, seeing her go, breaks free, and chases after ...

107   EXT. BOWLING ALLEY - DAY   107

Marie hurries to her car and gets in. Dan runs out,
disheveled, his lip cut.

                              DAN
                 Marie, no -- don't go -- !

                              MARIE
                 I don't know what we were thinking --

She starts the engine and rips out of the lot. Dan scrambles
toward his car. As he does, Jane emerges from the bowling
alley.

                              JANE
                 Dad, wait, what are you doing?

Dan hops in and guns the engine.

                          JANE (CONT'D)
                 DAD!

Dan floors it in reverse, flies out of the parking space
and...CRASH...

...collides with a car.

Dan looks back ...

Dan's POV: The familiar face of our Policeman stares back at
Dan. Beat. The Policeman sounds the siren and flashes the
lights.

108   EXT. BOWLING ALLEY - AN HOUR LATER   108

The rain has stopped.

The Police car is being lifted onto a flatbed truck.

Dan, flanked by Poppy, awaits his fate.

The Policeman walks up and hands Dan a summons.

                                                         (CONTINUED)

108 CONTINUED: 108

                              POLICEMAN
                    This is your summons for your court
                    appearance. One last thing -- you'll
                    need to surrender your license.

          And with that, Dan surrenders his license.

109 OMITTED   109

110 EXT. BEACH HOUSE - DAY   110

          Dan enters, followed by Poppy. He comes inside expecting the
          worst, but he doesn't expect to find ...

                              NANA
                         (with a forced smile)
                    Dan, you have some guests.

          Dan looks around the archway.

          Sitting in the living room - a WOMAN dressed in business
          attire and AN OLDER MAN in a suit.

                              DAN
                    Oh, hello.

          In this light, Dan looks like shit.

                              WOMAN
                    Hi, I'm Cindy Lamson, Editor of Special
                    Features for the Lamson Newspaper Group.

                              JAMES LAMSON
                    Jim Lamson, Publisher. It's a pleasure.

                              DAN
                    Nice to meet you.

                              CINDY LAMSON
                    We've been sitting here chatting with
                    your family. We've especially enjoyed
                    meeting your lovely daughters.

          Angle on Jane and Lilly. They are sitting dutifully on a
          small sofa. Jane seems somber and Lilly is near tears.

          Cara enters, carrying a tray with mugs of hot cider. She's
          wearing one of her trademark give-her-father-a-heart-attack
          outfits.

                                                              (CONTINUED)

                              CARA
                    Hot cider.

Cara serves the Lamsons first.   Then she crosses to Dan and
offers him a mug.

                              CARA (CONT'D)
                    Father --
                         (whispers into his ear)
                    Not only are you a murderer of love,
                    you're the worst parent ever.

Dan laughs, acting as if what Cara said was a joke.

                              CINDY LAMSON
                    That's sweet.

Cara crosses and sits with her sisters.

For Dan, the sight of his three girls sitting there is
excruciating.

Simultaneously, Mitch enters and sets a chair next to Dan.

                              CINDY LAMSON
                    As you know, we've met with two other
                    candidates, but we're confident that
                    we've saved the best for last.

                              MITCH
                    Ha.

                              DAN
                    Girls, you can go, if you'd like.

                              JAMES LAMSON, JR.
                    If it's alright, perhaps they should
                    stay. We like to keep the family
                    involved.

                              MITCH
                    Dan is all about keeping things in the
                    family. Aren't you, Dan?

Mitch puts his hand on Dan's knee. And squeezes.

                              CINDY LAMSON
                    That's why we're so drawn to you...your
                    honesty, your moral values, your
                    integrity. Your writing seems to
                    indicate the man you are. You're a
                    model. We have great plans for you. We
                    have 18 papers in 12 states.
                         (MORE)

                                                   (CONTINUED)

110   CONTINUED: (2)   110

                    CINDY LAMSON (cont'd)
          Overnight we'd increase your readership
          ten fold ...

                    JAMES LAMSON
          But basically what we do is try to do
          what you keep telling your readers to do:

                    CINDY LAMSON
          Family First. That's our mantra.

Dan can't take it anymore.

                    DAN
          Here's the thing:
               (Beat.)
          Somebody hasn't been reading his own
          column.

Beat. No one moves. Then --

                    CINDY LAMSON
          I'm not sure what that means.

111   INT. UPSTAIRS HALLWAY OUTSIDE THE GIRLS' ROOM   111

Dan's hand knocks on the door to the Girl's room.

The door opens slightly. Cara speaks through the crack.

                    CARA
          Go away. You're a liar! And a
          hypocrite! Cheating with your brother's
          girlfriend. And how long have you known
          her? Three days?! I'm never listening
          to you again.

Cara is joined by Jane.

                    JANE
          Two moving violations and a collision?
          Was that part of the plan?

                    CARA
               (returning)
          Worst of all -- you blew Lilly off.

                    JANE
          She's been wanting to show you something
          she made for you.

                    CARA
               (pointed)
          But you never showed up.

                                              (CONTINUED)

111   CONTINUED: 111

        Cara pushes the door shut.

        Lilly's project is slid out from under the door.

        Dan reaches down to pick it up as we hear the sound of a lock
        TURNING.

112   INT. BEACH HOUSE - STAIRCASE - DAY   112

        Dan slowly sits down on the steps. He opens Lilly's project.
        It's a homemade collage of old photos, decorated by hand.
        Photos of Dan and Suzanne on the beach. In the last photo,
        Suzanne holds a young girl, with Dan next to them and the
        Lighthouse in the background.

113   INT. BEACH HOUSE - KITCHEN - DAY   113

        Dan returns from upstairs, full of self-contempt. Poppy and
        Nana are making sandwiches. Dan holds up Lilly's collage
        They smile, knowingly, as if they've already seen it.

        Dan sets down Lilly's collage.

                        DAN (CONT'D)
                  (beat)
                I really messed up.

                        POPPY
                Well ...

                        NANA
                No, you didn't.

                        DAN
                Yeah, Mom, I did. My kids hate me and
                what I did to Lilly...

                        POPPY
                Don't forget Mitch ...

                        NANA
                John.

                        POPPY
                And those newspaper people ...

                        NANA
                Admittedly not a good day for you, Dan.

                                              (CONTINUED)

113 CONTINUED: 113

                              DAN
                    If I had just stayed focused on being
                    their dad --

                              NANA
                    Oh please. They're going to get over
                    this. Question is -- will you?

Beat. Dan can't answer.

                              NANA (CONT'D)
                    Love is messy.

                              DAN
                    But I should know better. I hurt my
                    kids.

                              NANA
                    So go un-hurt them.

Dan thinks. Then sighs ...

                              NANA (CONT'D)
                    Honey, you made some mistakes ...

                              POPPY
                    Many, so many --

                              NANA
                    But falling for Marie wasn't one of them.

114 INT. BEACH HOUSE - HALLWAY/STAIRWELL - DAY   114

On his way to the stairs, Dan is blind-sided by Mitch who
knocks Dan against the wall.

                              DAN
                    Mitch, I'm --

Angle on Mitch. His eyes are spider-web red.

                              MITCH
                    If it were anyone else ...

                              DAN
                    I'm -- uhm - so (sorry) --

A car horn BEEPS.

                              MITCH
                    Can you hold that thought?

                                                        (CONTINUED)

114   CONTINUED: 114

Mitch heads outside ...

Perplexed, Dan watches ...

Dan's POV: A fabulous red sports car pulls into the circular
drive. The tinted car window is lowered to reveal Ruthie
Draper. She calls out to Mitch ...

                    RUTHIE
          Get in, beautiful.

After Mitch opens the door and before he climbs in, he looks
back at Dan. Makes a fist. This fist gives way to something
softer, kinder. Then Mitch climbs in and they drive off.

And Dan continues up the stairs.

115   INT. BEACH HOUSE - GIRL'S ROOM - DAY   115

Dan tries the softest of knocks. Miraculously, the door
opens. He peeks in.

                    DAN
          Girls, I'd like to talk with Lilly alone,
          if I could.

Instead of leaving, Jane moves next to Lilly and sits. Cara
does the same on the other side.

Beat. *So that's how it's going to be.*

Dan gets down on his knees.

                    DAN (CONT'D)
          Okay, then all of you.
               (beat)
          I know I messed up big time.

                    CARA
          Yep.

                    JANE
          Yes, you did.

                    DAN
          Now, your mom.
               (to Lilly especially)
          I miss your mom. All the time. And I
          always will. But she's still here...

                    LILLY
          Mom's gone.

                                              (CONTINUED)

                              DAN
                No. She's still here. I see her
                everyday. I see her in your goodness,
                Jane, and, Cara, in your passion, and
                you...
                      (to Lilly)
                You have her eyes and her smile.
                      (beat)
                So here's what I'm gonna do. I'm
                grounding myself. For life.

Cara, especially, looks suspicious.

                              DAN (CONT'D)
                I am. I'm not going anywhere. I'm
                sticking with you. I will be with you --

                              LILLY
                You're with us every day.

                              DAN
                Well, I'm not going anywhere. See, I got
                a little confused -- with Marie -- but
                it's over. I lost my head -- got a
                little stupid because I love her. Wait,
                wait -- that's not what I mean. I don't
                love her. I mean, how could I? I've
                only known her...

                              CARA
                Three days.

                              DAN
                And how can you know in three days. But
                maybe you can. Maybe sometimes you just
                know, you know. I don't know. I love
                her Iloveher Iloveher Iloveher --

                              JANE
                      (beat)
                Then go get her.

Beat. *What?*

                              CARA
                We so prefer her to you.

Beat. Dan looks to Lilly. She moves forward.

                              LILLY
                Go.

115   CONTINUED: (2)   115

        But Dan can't move. Lilly leans forward and whispers in his
        ear.

                              LILLY (CONT'D)
                    Now.

        Dan and Lilly hug tightly.

116   INT. BEACH HOUSE - STAIRWELL - DAY   116

        Dan races down the stairs. As he heads toward the front
        door, Poppy tosses him his coat.

        And he's handed a sack lunch by Nana who says, "For the
        road."

117   EXT. BEACH HOUSE - CONTINUOUS   117

        Dan exits the house and heads toward the car. Poppy trails
        after.

        Dan pulls out his car keys and then stops.

                              POPPY
                    What? What is it?

                              DAN
                    I can't do it.

                              POPPY
                    You must.

                              DAN
                    I can't! I don't have a license!

        The front door swings open. Dan stops, looks back at ...

        Jane, who smiles slightly.

        As Jane passes by, Dan hands her the keys.

        Next comes Lilly ...

                              LILLY
                    I'm pretty good with maps.

        This leaves only Cara who says...

                                                        (CONTINUED)

117   CONTINUED: 117

                              CARA
                 This is so queer.
                      (with complete sincerity)
                 But I wouldn't miss it for anything ...

Dan heads to the car to join his family.

118   EXT. BEACH HOUSE - MOMENTS LATER   118

The Camera pulls back and up as the extended family sends Dan
and his daughters on their way. Their hastily packed bags
are loaded in the back of the car. Off they go.

                              DAN (V.O.)
                 Dear Readers, for most of you, this is my
                 first column in your paper.

118A   EXT. NEW YORK CITY - BRIDGE - DAY   118A

Pavement racing past.

Camera pans up...

With Jane at the wheel, the Burns' car drives over a bridge
into Manhattan.

                              DAN (V.O.)
                 Normally, I will be answering your
                 questions but today I want to break from
                 my usual format and talk to you about the
                 subject of plans. Not so much my plans
                 for this column. More like life plans.

       SCENES 119-127 OMITTED

127A   EXT. FITNESS GYM - NIGHT   127A

                              DAN (V.O.)
                 How we all make them. And how we hope
                 that our kids make good smart safe plans
                 of their own.

Dan walks along a bank of windows searching for...

                              DAN (V.O.) (CONT'D)
                 But, if we're really honest with
                 ourselves, most of the time our plans
                 don't work out as we hoped.
                      (MORE)

(CONTINUED)

127A CONTINUED: 127A

> DAN (V.O.) (CONT'D)
> *So instead of asking our young people*
> *"What are your plans?" "What do you plan*
> *to do with your life?" Maybe we could*
> *tell them this --*

He stops when he sees...

Marie running on a treadmill, not seeing Dan.

> DAN (V.O.) (CONT'D)
> *Plan to be surprised.*

Then Marie looks up and sees Dan and his daughters in the
window.

She smiles in disbelief. She stops running.

On Dan, happy.

                                          SCREEN TO BLACK:

OVER CREDITS

128 EXT. BEACH HOUSE - BACK YARD - DAY   128

A band begins to play. (Sondre Lerche and the Face Down
Quartet dressed in baby blue tuxedos.)

Dan, in a suit, and Marie, in a wedding dress, step onto the
porch.

As the first notes of Sondre Lerche's MODERN NATURE are
played, Dan and Marie come down the porch steps.

Guests arrive from all directions, until the yard is full.

Dan and Marie move onto the dance floor. Others join in.

And we pull away and go up - up - up as the family dances.

Q & A

WITH PETER HEDGES
BY ROB FELD

So, to start, **Dan in Real Life** *came to you as a rewrite through Disney, correct? As opposed to* **Pieces of April,** *which was your own spec.*

PETER HEDGES: I owed Disney four weeks of work. The project I had been rewriting wasn't going well. So I offered to pay them back, but Nina Jacobson and Brad Epstein, who I had worked with on *About a Boy* when he was at Tribeca, sent me a box of scripts that were in development at the studio and told me to pick one to work on. The second script I read was Pierce Gardner's *Dan in Real Life,* and I didn't need to read any more scripts. I thought that the story aligned with my sensibilities—it's a story I wish I had thought up—and I felt like it was a script I could help. I set out to work for four weeks and that four weeks turned into five months, and I remember the writing process being very relaxed. I would start each day with the screenplay, would work only to the point that I was satisfied, and then would stop. It felt easy in a way that writing hadn't felt for a long time. I had no hopes other than that I was being helpful, but when I turned in the script a flurry of calls came quickly. I was a bit stunned by what ended up happening: Nina called and said that she was green-lighting the film and that I could cast whomever I wanted. I said, "You're letting a writer cast a film?" and she said, "Oh, you're going to direct it." And I said no because I had other

---

Rob Feld interviewed Peter Hedges in Brooklyn on October 17, 2007. Feld is a screenwriter and independent producer at Manifesto Films. His writings on film and interviews with such noted filmmakers as James L. Brooks, Charlie Kaufman, Bill Condon, Peter Hedges, Noah Baumbach, Mike Nichols, and Alexander Payne appear regularly in *Written By* magazine and *DGA Quarterly,* as well as in the Newmarket Shooting Script® series.

projects and I didn't think this was a good idea. But she insisted that it was a good idea and I set out to see if she was a person of her word, which she was; she let me cast Steve Carell and Juliette Binoche, and that is how it all started.

What shape was the script in when you got it? Where did you think it had to be taken?

PH: I felt that Pierce had written a really fun family film. My first goal was to retain whatever of his work that I could—mainly because I liked his script, but also because it's what I hope people who rewrite me will do. It just seems like good manners. I have been rewritten where I feel writers do everything they can to eradicate anything I contributed, and other times I have been rewritten where I feel like they built on what I had done. In this instance, I wanted the story to be an adult love story– which is different from a family film. I wanted it to be a film for adults, but that children could see and quite possibly enjoy. So for me it was simply about making it about two adults who are doing everything they can *not* to fall in love.

Was the structure basically the same?

PH: Yes, although originally it took place over more days around Christmastime. I wanted to avoid the holidays and for the story to take place over three days, which is how long it took for Cara to fall in love with Marty. Also, it used to be that they lived in California and they flew to New Jersey; I have them live in New Jersey and drive to Rhode Island.

Was Jane's driving subplot not there?

PH: No, she always wanted to drive.

So was your task to darken it up, make it a bit more adult?

PH: Darken it, deepen it in places, turn it from a family sex farce into an adult love story. That was the basic idea. The title was a tremendous gift, because every time I would work on scenes, or certainly as we were making the film, we would always ask the question, "Did that feel real? Believable? Truthful?" To go from making *Pieces of April* on a shoestring budget to a film with a much greater one, in a climate where many of the films of this genre are made in broader strokes than perhaps the human comedies I would like to make—having the touchstone of the title was helpful. So a lot of my work was to get the script to a place where it met my criteria for what feels believable. Everyone has their bar or their limit, and mine is that I love stories where believable characters do unbelievable things. That was the work for me, making sure moments felt grounded. And I suppose to making everything harder for Dan.

At the same time, one of the things that Pierce had done, which really appealed to me and I wanted to keep intact, was that he knew it was Dan's story; that this wasn't an equal opportunity film where every character in the family needed a big moment; that the family was almost a character unto itself. As a person who worked for years on the novel and then the screenplay of *What's Eating Gilbert Grape* and did *Pieces of April*, I had been dining out on dysfunction for more than a decade. I liked the idea that this wasn't a story about a dysfunctional family—there are actually, somewhere in America, a few families that get along. This was to be one of those families. This was not to be a collection of freaks and misfits, which is my favorite thing to do. This family would stand in contrast to Dan's lostness, his emptiness. It would be a movie about a guy who was stuck, a guy whose heart had frozen over and who was doing the best he could to get through each day.

In my own life, I was raised by my dad. So it was important to me that we get the truth of being a single parent—not in a maudlin or overwrought way, but in a real way. I called my dad when I started work on the script and asked, "What do you remember about being a single parent? What was hard? What was good?" And he said, "The hardest times were the middle-of-the-night times." So I came up with that opening moment where he rolls over and there she *isn't*. That was an important scene for me. A quiet moment that would hopefully play quite real. He also said, "There was no time as a single parent to feel sorry for yourself. I probably wanted to, but I couldn't." There is nothing more unattractive than a film character who feels sorry for himself, unless the person is, I suppose, ultra attractive, perhaps naked, and about to break into song or something. But anyway, that was helpful to me. I asked, "When were you happiest?" And he said, "Making your lunch." He loved making our lunches.

When we were shooting that scene, I told Steve to make a different sandwich for each daughter. I suggested he do something extra-special for his middle daughter, as she was the one Dan was struggling with the most. Steve came up with that beautiful moment where he squirts the honey on the middle sandwich, and he didn't even make it a smiley face; the mouth is a straight line.

113

While editing, Sarah Flack and I wrestled a lot with the first reel of the film. We cut many of the early scenes in an attempt to get to the house earlier. Still, the first reel feels slow to me.

Steve is very fond of the first reel because he says he feels it lets the audience know that this isn't going to be a big laugh-out-loud, ha-ha funny movie, and that they need to be patient, come along and the laughs will come later. My appreciation for the reel, those first ten or twelve minutes, is growing. Mostly, though, in the beginning of the script, I wanted to make sure I wasn't violating the *real life* aspect of Pierce's title.

I was also going to say, along with the uncharacteristically functional family, it didn't have that sense of impending doom that you so frequently do. The death had happened already.

PH: Right. I am a great lover of the gathering storm or the untold secret, and I guess for me that was also staying true to Pierce's original intentions. My fear, always, particularly after I was asked to direct the film, was that it wasn't enough; the story wasn't enough. It confused me at first when I got the response to the rewrite from my agents and from the studio, because I wasn't really in a position of sitting in judgment of the work. I felt that I had done more than what I had been asked to do and that I had helped, but I never imagined that I'd direct it.

And turning it into something else entirely would really be someone else's decision.

PH: Right. But I write everything in such a way so as I would like to direct it, knowing that I most likely won't even get the chance. It just makes me invest more. It feels only fair to write something that you wouldn't mind directing yourself. So I worried, as I do about all the stories I seem to get myself mixed up in, if this one was enough. The stories I tell tend to be small stories, which means they must be done beautifully or there isn't much use for them.

I was walking down the street soon after the studio asked me to direct *Dan in Real Life*. I ran into a friend who said I looked worried. I said, "I'm confused. I turned in this script and they would like me to direct it, and I don't think it's about enough." And she asked, "What is it about?" I started to tell her that it was about this man who had lost the love of his life and about whether he can find love again, and I stopped because I realized I was talking to my friend who had lost her husband in 9/11 and who was raising three boys alone. When I caught myself, she reached over and patted my hand and said, "It's about enough."

And this notion of surprise…

PH: In 1993, I was to give the commencement speech at the North Carolina School of the Arts, my alma mater, and I had no speech to give. I arrived a couple of days early, looking for a speech. I wandered the campus and ran into a student who was about to graduate. She was in a panic, I asked what was wrong, and she said, "My parents keep asking me what I plan to do with my life, and I don't know what to tell them." In a moment of hubris, I said, "I will deal with your parents." And I built an entire speech about plans: how I had gone to this school, how I had planned to be an actor and it didn't work out, and then I planned to do this, and I planned to do that, and my general premise was, "I am standing here today because my plan failed." At the end of the speech I said, "When your parents ask you what you want to do with your life and you are tired of giving an answer, you don't know the answer—and it is perfectly okay to not know the answer—consider saying this: Plan to be surprised."

The whole experience of this process was a surprise and as I was working, I thought, "Oh, this is the kind of thing Dan would say in a column." Originally, both Pierce and I had quite a bit of voiceover at the beginning of the script. Dan's column helped set it up, but it always felt pedestrian to me. It just felt like we had seen it before. I love voiceover. It can be great. But in this instance, it felt like what we really needed to do was not hear him tell us about his life; we needed to see his life. In the final voiceover, Pierce had echoed a theme of surprise and I found myself drawing upon this notion of "plan to be surprised." When I brought that phrase to the project, it became a real touchstone. The touchstones were *real life*, Marie's notion of *human funny* in the bookstore, and *plan to be surprised*.

Where the "plan to be surprised" notion was helpful in the writing of the script and the making of the film is that I basically try to create circumstances wherein we will be surprised, wherein something unexpected, and hopefully wonderful, can happen. I don't think the story of this film is anything revolutionary. It is sweet, it is simple. Increasingly I think the simple stories are the most interesting to watch on film, or most satisfying for me to write. I have writer friends to whom a simple story would induce a heart attack. They need the cross narratives and the time jumps and the fractured, nonlinear miasma. But for me, I liked the deceptively simple story that

Pierce created. At the same time, it then requires everything be exquisite. Of course, that is a subjective notion and you can only go with your own taste or the taste of the people with whom you work, but that is what we set out to do. I kept going back to real life—does this feel real? Not necessarily real as in everyone will recognize it, but will people be able to believe it? In retrospect, I missed some chances to ground the film in a more believable way. Too many big group scenes, perhaps too much familial happiness. Oh, well.

After working as an indie filmmaker, how was your experience with a big studio?

PH: Amazing, actually. We were in pre-production when I got the call that Nina had been replaced, and for me it was a dark moment. She had given me a kind of permission to make my kind of movie at the studio. I can't imagine that I would have wandered down this road without the assurance that someone like Nina Jacobson had my back. But we had our cast, we were picking locations, and Nina was suddenly gone. About that time, Dianne Dreyer, my longtime collaborator, called me up and said, "Peter, I remember you used to say about *Pieces of April* that it was a film that you *had* to make. Now, I just reread *Dan in Real Life* and I know you want to make it, and I know you can't wait to make it, but I don't know if you have answered yet why you *have* to make it."

And that question, coming from that person at that particular moment, was like a dagger to my heart. My crucible moment, along with Nina's leaving Disney. Those two things collided. I locked myself in my house in Brooklyn, my family was away, and for three days I didn't take a phone call. I made note after note after note, I walked around the house and kept asking the question, "Why this movie? Why this movie?" And then I had one of those moments where you feel like you should actually have a career in marketing, because I came up with this question, "How do we find love again?" It sounds sappy now, but at the moment it felt profound. "How do we find love again?" And then an answer came. "You don't. But if you are lucky, every so often, love will find you." It was a Hallmark-ish moment, perhaps, but at that moment it was what I had to do: Nina was gone, Dianne was telling me that this movie doesn't mean to me what *Pieces of April* did, and I know from experience that my strength comes from whom and what I love. If I don't have a complete ache and burning to tell a story, I am probably not going to do a good job.

Then I embarked on a very intense private period where I rewrote and rewrote the script because I was nervous that I didn't have my protector at the studio. I worked around the clock. I thought the movie was too attractive for the studio not to make at this point—with Steve, Dane, Juliette—and they were going to want it to become something that I couldn't make it be. I was convinced. So the day I finished what would be the shooting draft of the script, I got a call that Oren Aviv, the man who replaced Nina, wanted to meet me for lunch. I had finished the script at about four in the morning and I went to meet him in a restaurant in New York six or seven hours later. I hadn't slept and as I was entering the restaurant, I caught my reflection in the window, and literally my eyes were in line with my mouth, puffy and swollen, and I thought I could not be in a worse position to meet him and defend something. I sat down and told him that this was awkward for me, and we started to talk and very quickly I realized in this conversation that I had a partner on this film; that he was going to have my back, as it were. Oren very much wanted me to make my kind of film and, even better, he made sure it was possible.

My reality was thematically mirroring my movie again. *Pieces of April* was about people running out of time while we didn't have enough time to make the movie. With *Dan in Real Life* I was making a film about how we find love again, and you don't, love finds you—so here I was, making a movie now for a big studio, only able to carry over two or three people from *Pieces of April* for various reasons, in a new world with a new boss, if you will, and to my surprise, I was able to find love again. The very thing that the movie was about actually happened to me. This has actually been as ideal of an experience with a studio as one could ever have. Where the surprise continues to this day for me is that I made a certain set of assumptions based on twenty-four years of doing this, that if you work for a studio, they are going to water down your vision, they are going to seize your film, they are going to recut it, and hopefully you will have a big enough career that in a few years you can release the director's cut. Well, there is no director's cut to be released, because the director's cut is the cut that is in the theaters. Of course, I had the good fortune that Steve Carell wanted to make the same kind of film I did.

So surprise seemed like an appropriate theme to kind of guide not only the telling of what the story is—Dan is surprised by meeting her, by what he does, that he does find love again—but also because I was surprised that it was possible, within the structure of a big studio and the demands that commercial filmmaking entail, to make a personal film in a very particular way and have it be embraced. It is hard for me to claim it, because so many of my friends who have labored like I did in the independent world don't want to believe that it's possible, but in this case it is the truth. You don't have to like the film, but I can tell you that any filmmaker would like to have the experience I got to have making it.

We touched on this before, but I wanted to talk about the opening moment of a film, which is always a struggle.

PH: Always. I keep starting movies with people waking up and I've got to come up with something new. I spent a great deal of my time rewriting the first fifteen pages of the movie. I think I still write more like a novelist, so I want to layer everything, kind of drop it in and let it build, and I think it is harder and harder in this culture where, if it hasn't grabbed you by the throat ten minutes in, you're changing the channel. It's a struggle. But again, I ultimately kept going back to where Dan ends up—standing in a window with his girls, looking at the woman he's begun to love. I didn't want to start with him writing a column because to me, if he starts writing a column, it's a movie about a columnist. To me this is a movie about a man who happens to be a columnist. But what's more important, that he's a columnist or that he's alone? Since the movie closes with him finding love, let's start with the truth, and the truth is he's alone. How can we know that without being told it? You see that the other side of the bed has all this stuff on it. You don't know why. It is always a struggle when writing—and increasingly I am convinced that good writing is what you don't write—to find what is the least amount of story and moments that you need to tell the story, and that is always a long process for me, figuring it out.

That moment where he pulls himself up and says "All right" is so key, like he's making a deal with himself to face the day.

PH: It does say a lot about him. It was the last take and I just said, "Can you say, 'All right' or 'Okay'? Something that makes me feel like the day starts." Boom, he nailed it and we moved on from there.

You have to buy into Dan from the get-go. At what point do you think the audience makes its deal with Dan, "Okay, we're with you." What is the key to him?

PH: That is a great question. Some people say to me, "I get him when he is making the sandwiches, or when he is folding the underwear." For my dad, he gets him the moment he rolls over and his wife is not there. For me, it is when he puts Cara in the car, says, "You can't know love. You don't love him," backs up, and he drives off. The boy moves across the window and she is pressed against the glass, and Dan gives that look of, "How much longer am I going to be able to keep this together?"

You set up echoes and made it into something.

PH: Yeah, the Lasse Hallström influence. There are a lot of echoes in *Gilbert Grape* and whenever we would come up with a line or a moment that could be an echo, Lasse would get so happy. In fact, there is one scene near the end of *Gilbert Grape* where three echoes occur. It's almost shameless, but it works. You listen to a great piece of classical music—not that this movie is at that level—and something recurs and it just feels familiar, and then if it recurs and it actually means more, it accrues a kind of heft and a kind of power. So, yeah. Which ones come to mind?

Well, there's "I made it up," for one. Both Lilly and Marty say it.

PH: Oh, I never realized that one.... That was an echo I wasn't even aware of. Ruthie has an echo or two. "Sometimes you just know, you know." Dan does a deliberate echo when he says to Marie, "There is a certain rightness to our wrongness." And then, of course, Dan's "I love her, I love her, I love her" late in script.

It's ideas repeating with change.

PH: Those are so important because he is telling his daughter from the beginning, "You don't know what love is." And what love does to any of us, is it humbles us, and in this case, Dan is humbled by the fact that the words that best describe how he ultimately feels are the same words that his daughter, just a few days earlier, had used to describe how she felt. It just felt like the best way to communicate what is true, and that is that children teach you, if you let them.

You had a huge cast to juggle, something you had not done before.

PH: Twenty-seven scenes with nineteen actors, not extras, and ten of them are children, shooting on a practical set, which means your shooting day is shortened by the mere fact that the sun doesn't want to work as long as you do.

We had a very narrow window of time in which to make the film because *The Office* shut down in mid-season for two and a half months so Steve could come do this film. Part of why I wanted to direct *Dan in Real Life* was that when I think about *Pieces of April*, one of the happiest times was the period when I had Patty Clarkson, Oliver Platt, John Gallagher, Jr., Alison Pill, and Alice Drummond in that car. I had the same actors for five days and it was all in the car, and when I thought about doing this movie, I thought, "Oh, this is nineteen actors in a house." It's the same idea. Since I really only want to direct films because I love working with actors, it seemed like this would be a great experience, with everybody around all the time. The first big group scenes I directed, I directed quite terribly, I think, but I got better at it. My DP Larry Sher and others would come on weekends, and we would walk around the house and figure out where we could put people in a general sense. You block in the adults and hold as long as possible before you bring in the kids, because they can only work a certain number of hours each day.

Even more difficult is trying to make it feel natural, which really comes down to casting. Amy Ryan, Jessica Hecht, Norbert Leo Butz, Frank Wood—Tony winners and nominees all throughout the movie. I basically explained that they would be underused. I openly admit that I overcast this film. I wanted every actor in this movie to be great, to be the best that we could find. I promised that opportunities for moments would come up with the way we were shooting this movie, but ultimately we are not going to understand your character, we are not going to know each of their stories, but if *you* do, and *we* do within ourselves, we will feel it and they won't feel like cardboard cutouts. I purposely cast people who were theater-based because in the theater you have to learn very quickly that your job is to serve the play. Once all these people arrived, they were so delighted to be amongst each other. We had to build the family without Steve because he came in about midnight before the first day of shooting and I think his call was at five-thirty a.m. He had been filming his show up until the last moment. He wanted to be there, but it was not possible. I had to go to all the actors and say, "Look, we are going to rehearse this film in an unconventional way. Dan is in every scene but we are going to rehearse without him. We are going to build a family and he is going to enter it."

We cooked meals together, did improvisations, under my supervision they put together a talent show for Steve/Dan, so when he met them for the first time, he sat in a chair and everyone sang songs and read letters to him. All the letters to him started with, "Dan, you may not remember this, but …" Norbert and Amy decided that their characters had had a shotgun wedding because they were pregnant. Dane wrote a great story about how his first girl-friend had been in love with Dan and when he brought her home and Dan realized that she was interested in him, Dan did all these things to dissuade her from liking him. Mitch was really grateful that Dan had his back, and Steve is hearing this letter read to him like, "Ugh." I had Dane sing, "Did you ever know that you are my hero? You are the wind beneath my wings." Norbert and Jessica Hecht sang, "He Ain't Heavy, He's My Brother." The girls sang the Sister Sledge song "We Are Family." Dianne Wiest and John Mahoney sang "Forever Young."

So the hardest part of making this film in terms of those actors was that I had a bunch of racehorses and I needed to hold them back. But they understood. You don't get many opportunities to be around so many terrific people, and everybody made a sacrifice. All the actors worked for less than they should be paid, which allowed us to keep the cost of the film down, but it also was that sense of sacrifice that makes a movie special. You invest more in it. You commit more to it because you are more determined to make it a great experience.

John Mahoney was one of the last actors to join the cast. I remember I was taking a train to Long Island the morning John received the script. He started reading at nine a.m. and by eleven a.m. that same day I was on the phone with him. I said, "John, before you say anything, I just want you to know that I am still working on the script, and that if you will do this film, I will make the part better for you." And he said, "Don't." I said, "I'm sorry?" He said, "Don't. I read this script. I understand the story. I love the character. It doesn't need to be any bigger. Actors like me look for a long, long time for projects like this one. When you have been around as long as I have and they come around, you know that you want to be a part of it." When you have an actor of John's caliber say those words, you go, "Damn, this is a dream."

What were the landmines for this movie?

PH: There were many. For starters, the basic premise. The setup, as it were. If you don't buy the setup, we're in trouble. I thought if you don't feel in the bookstore scene that these two people have a deep connection—not a surface connection, not just a sexual or flirtatious connection—if there isn't something deeper going on, then there isn't much use for this movie. Then it is just two people who are sneaking around, hot for each other. Not interesting. Another big one was the "Go Now" scene at the end. That needed to feel especially real. I was also particularly nervous about the shower scene because I thought it was bordering on unbelievable. Anything that bordered on unbelievable or maudlin felt troubling to me, but I think it was also this overall sense that if there wasn't enough ache/pain/longing running under everything Dan does, then it would just seem too easy. Also, finding the balance with the family—not a dysfunctional family but also not a perfect, idyllic family. If I could do it all over again, I would probably swap out one or two family activities for a family chore or two. I would like to have a little less of the "Oh, here we go doing another fun thing together." I would probably change that if I could.

Another scene I knew we had to land is one of my favorites, both in how it is written and how it was shot—where Dan is forced to do the dishes after insulting his brother in front of the family and his new girl-friend. Mitch arrives to help him. Dan wants to explain that he met Marie before and tell the truth, but Mitch interrupts and says, "I feel things for this girl that I have never felt before."

Did Steve and Dane know each other from before?

PH: They had met once, briefly. Dane had an awe-like admiration for Steve, which is part of why I cast him. I thought if he could bring that feel-ing to the movie, it would make it all the more difficult for Dan. All the more painful. I thought this scene, while it read well, could play soupy, it could play broad, and when we found where to shoot it and how to shoot it, from a distance, as if we are peeking in, just let those two guys have a quiet, sin-cere conversation, it felt to me like a very important moment. It says to their fans that they are not going to do what you expect them to do, but if you listen and watch them, what they are going to do is something lovely. Because they play the scene simply and sincerely, we feel like we're watch-ing something very real.

The rock-throwing moment. It was a way to immediately visualize how he was feeling, sans dialogue.

PH: It is also an argument for shooting whenever possible on a practical location. There used to be a big sequence where Dan tried to eat a bunch of food and he spits it out, and we cut that scene. Then there was a scene where he confronts Marie on the porch in front of the family; it was very caustic and it felt interesting, but it just wasn't of this movie. One scene felt too broad and the other too aggressive. I kept looking at that beach, which was so beautiful. I thought, "This is a crime, it's right here." Literally the last day we had everybody, we had more work to do on a particular scene and I said, "We have got to go outside right now." It was lunchtime and I will never forget, people literally sprinting with cameras, everybody running, and I still didn't know how I was going to do the scene. We got out there, figured it out, and it was another example of *Pieces of April*-ing it. That scene does not exist in written form, though I wrote it out for the shooting script. I'm really happy with it.

I am going to close by throwing one more quote back at you, which was, "If I aspire to anything, it is to tell stories that are easy to understand but hard to handle."

PH: Yeah. This story is not so hard to handle. I failed there. In this instance I would hearken back to what I said earlier. I wanted to make a film for adults that my kids could see. It was very important to me, if I was going to be away from my family the amount of time that I had to be to make this film, then I wanted to make something that I could share with them. In this case, I felt like if I had come up with this story, it would have probably been darker than the story that Pierce created, but I felt to impose my kind of inherent darkness onto this film would be a violation of his story and wouldn't necessarily serve it, either. I did try to inject an undertone of Dan's sadness and grief throughout the story, and that would be the hard-to-handle element. It is not hard to handle in the deeper way my other films may be. But that was a conscious choice to make a joy-based movie, which reminds me of what my late, great teacher, Sanford Meisner, used to say: "Make a choice and accept the consequences."

CAST AND CREW CREDITS

TOUCHSTONE PICTURES and FOCUS FEATURES
present A JON SHESTACK Production

DAN IN REAL LIFE

STEVE CARELL   JULIETTE BINOCHE   DANE COOK   JOHN MAHONEY   EMILY BLUNT
ALISON PILL   BRITTANY ROBERTSON   MARLENE LAWSTON   AMY RYAN
NORBERT LEO BUTZ   JESSICA HECHT   FRANK WOOD   and   DIANNE WIEST

Casting by BERNARD TELSEY, C.S.A.	Film Editor SARAH FLACK, A.C.E.	Produced by BRAD EPSTEIN
Music Supervisor DANA SANO	Production Designer SARAH KNOWLES	Written by PIERCE GARDNER and PETER HEDGES
Co-Producer DIANNE DREYER	Director of Photography LAWRENCE SHER	Directed by PETER HEDGES
Music by SONDRE LERCHE	Executive Producers NOAH ROSEN and DARLENE CAAMAÑO LOQUET MARI JO WINKLER- IOFFREDA	Unit Production Manager MARI JO WINKLER- IOFFREDA
Original Songs Written and Performed by SONDRE LERCHE		First Assistant Director STEPHEN DUNN
Costume Designer ALIX FRIEDBERG	Produced by JON SHESTACK	Second Assistant Director PAUL PRENDERVILLE

CAST
(In order of appearance)

Dan . . . . STEVE CARELL
Marie . . . . JULIETTE BINOCHE
Mitch . . . . DANE COOK
Jane . . . . ALISON PILL
Cara . . . . . BRITTANY ROBERTSON
Lilly . . . . . . MARLENE LAWSTON
Nana . . . . DIANNE WIEST
Poppy . . . . JOHN MAHONEY
Clay . . . . NORBERT LEO BUTZ
Eileen . . . . AMY RYAN
Amy . . . . JESSICA HECHT
Howard . . . . FRANK WOOD
Will . . . . HENRY MILLER
Rachel . . . . ELLA MILLER
Elliot . . . . . . CAMERON "CJ" ADAMS
Jessica . . . . JESSICA LUSSIER
Gus . . . . SETH D'ANTUONO
Olivia . . . . MARGOT JANSON
Bella . . WILLA CUTHRELL-TUTTLEMAN
Ruthie Draper . . . . . . EMILY BLUNT
Marty Barasco . . . . . . FELIPE DIEPPA
Policeman . . . MATTHEW MORRISON

James Lamson . . . BERNIE McINERNEY
Cindy Lamson . . . . AMY LANDECKER
Bookstore Clerk . . . . . STEVE MELLOR
Bowling Alley Manager . . PAULINE GREGORY
Suzanne Burns . . . . . . SHANA CARR
Jane (Age 13) . . . . . NICOLE MORIN
Cara (Age 11) . . . CHARLOTTE DAVIES
Lilly (Age 4) . . . . ZOE PAULKIS
Lilly's Dance Partner . . . LUCAS HEDGES
As Himself . . . . . . SONDRE LERCHE
Wedding Band . . . . THE FACES DOWN:
KATO ÅDLAND-Guitar
OLE LUDVIG KRÜGER-Drums
MORTEN SKAGE-Bass
Wedding Singer . . . . MARCI OCCHINO
Helicopter Pilot . . . . . . MIKE PEAVEY
Stunt Coordinator . . . RICK SORDELET
"Dan" Stunt Double . . . . ERIK SOLKY
"Marie" Stunt Double . SABINE VARNES
Stunt Players . . CHICK BERNHARD, ROSIE
BERNHARD, JARED BURKE, BARBARA
LEE-BELMONTE, PAUL MARINI, TINA
McKISSICK, JEFF MEDEIROS, ANTHONY
MOLINARI, DINO MUCCIO

Stunt Drivers . . . . . . CHRIS BARNES
SHAWNNA THIBODEAU
Casting Associate
. . . . . TIFFANY LITTLE CANFIELD
Script Supervisor . . . DIANNE DREYER
Associate Producer . . . GINNY BREWER
Production Supervisor . . . . . ERICA KAY
Art Director . . . . . MARK E. GARNER
Set Designer . GEOFFREY S. GRIMSMAN
Set Decorator
. . . . . KYRA FRIEDMAN-CURCIO
Construction Coordinator
. . . . JOSEPH KEARNEY
Leadman . . . . RICHARD BRUNTON
Buyers . . . . MORGAN KLING
GRETCHEN SCHLOTTMAN
On-Set Dresser . . . . ADAM ROFFMAN
Additional On-Set Dresser . . ROB CHALK
Set Dressing Gang Boss
. . . . . . BRENNER HUGH HARRIS
Draper . . . . . MARILYN SALVATORE
Set Dressers . . . . GUY BREMEL,
HOLLY LAWS, TIMOTHY LEWIS,
MARK O'NEILL
Art Department Coordinator
. . . . J.M. HUNTER
Graphic Artists
. . . . EDWARD A. IOFFREDA
KATHERINE TOWER
Art Department PA
. . . . ASHLEIGH STANCZAK
Costume Supervisor . . . . HOPE SLEPAK
Key Set Costumer
. . . . TARYN WALSH WEAVER
Costumer . . . . MOLLY O'HAVER
Set Costumers . . . . . MAILI LAFAYETTE
PARRISH KENNINGTON
Additional Costumer . . . SARAH MINK
Tailor . . . . JODI B. STONE
Stitcher . . . . JANNA PEDERSON
Costume PA . . . BARBARA ROTUNDO
A Camera Operator . . . . . DAN GOLD
First Assistant Camera . . JULIE DONOVAN
Second Assistant Camera
. . . . BRYAN G. HAIGH
B Camera/Steadicam Operator
. . . . . FAIRES ANDERSON SEKIYA
B Camera First Assistant
. . . . PETER KUTTNER
B Camera Second Assistant
. . . . THOM WILLEY
Additional First Assistant Cameras
. . . . WILLIAM FLOYD
SCOTT MAGUIRE

Film Loader . . . . . SUZANNE DIETZ
Aerial Unit Director of Photography
. . . . DAVE NORRIS
2nd Unit Director of Photography
. . . . ROBERT BAROCCI
Unit Still Photographer . . . MERIE WEIS-
MILLER WALLACE, SMPSP
Camera PA . . . MICHAEL KOWALCZYK
Video Assist Operator
. . . . CHARLES LAUGHON
Production Sound Mixer
. . . . JOHN PRITCHETT, C.A.S.
Boom Operator . . . DAVID M. ROBERTS
Sound Utility/Additional Boom Operator
. . . . KELLY DORAN
Makeup Department Head
. . . . LUANN CLAPS
Key Makeup Artist . . . . MATIKI ANOFF
Makeup Artist . . . . . . TRISH SEENEY
Hair Department Head . . NATHAN J. BUSCH
Hairstylist to Ms. Binoche
. . . . ALAN D'ANGERIO
Key Hairstylist . . . . JOHN JAMES
Hairstylist
. . EMMA LaCARBONARA ROTONDI
Additional Set Dressers
. . . . TIM ROWCROFT
TIMANDRA ALYS VINCENT
Set Decorating PA . . SHAUNA SANCHEZ
Production Coordinator
. . . . SUSAN EHRHART
Assistant Production Coordinator
. . . . SARAH CONNOLLY
Assist. Production Coordinator/Travel
. . . . MARIE RODRIGUEZ
Production Secretary
. . . . KATIE M. MURPHY
Dailies Coordinator . . LINDSAY JAEGER
Office PAs . . . . KEVIN LANG
JON SCHERMERHORN
Film Courier . . . . JEFF PINETTE
Production Intern . . . DANIEL STANGL
Location Manager . . MARIA T. BIERNIAK
Assistant Location Manager
. . . . IAN MacGREGOR
Locations Assistant . . . . . EOIN WALSH
Location Scouts . . . . LAURA BERNING,
ANN KIKER, KIP MYERS,
BEN THOMAS
Locations PA . . . . . . JASON QUIMBY
Production Accountant
. . . . KENNETH J. LAFAYETTE
First Assistant Accountant
. . . . MICHAEL JOHNSON

Second Assistant Accountant
. . . . MARCI GRABER
Second Assistant Accountant
. . . . JOANNA SPEARS
Payroll Accountant . . . . . FELIX CHEN
Accounting Clerk. . LINDSAY MEDEIROS
Post Production Accountants
. . . . MICHELLE SARAMA
                    DIANA ASCHER
            TREVANNA POST, Inc.
Post Production Supervisor
. . . . JENNIFER LANE
Post Production Coordinator
. . . . ALEXIS WISCOMB
First Assistant Editor. . . JANET GAYNOR
Post Production Assistant . . . . JEN CHOI
Re-Recording Mixers
. . . . ROBERTO FERNANDEZ
              DOMINICK TAVELLA
Re-Recorded at . . SOUND ONE CORP.
Supervising Music Editor
. . . . SHARI L. JOHANSON
Assistant Music Editors . . MIKE PATRICK
                    DEBORA LILAVOIS
Supervising Sound Editor . . ELIZA PALEY
Assistant Sound Editor . . IGOR NIKOLIĆ
Dialogue Editor . . . . LAURA CIVIELLO
Sound Editor . . . . . GERALD DONLAN
Sound Effects Editor . . HEATHER GROSS
ADR Editor . . . . . . JANE McCULLEY
Foley Supervisor . . WILLIAM SWEENEY
Foley Artist. . . . . JACK PECK
Sound Effects Recordists
. . . . ERIC STRAUSSER
                      ERIC POTTER
Foley Recordist. . . . . RYAN COLLISON
ADR Mixer . . . . . BOBBY JOHANSON
ADR Recordist
. . . . . . KRISSOPHER CHEVANNES
Re-Recordists . . . . . DROR GESCHEIT
                    HARRY HIGGINS
Mix Technicians . . . . . BOB TROELLER
                      AVI LANIADO
Dolby® Consultant . . STEVE F. B. SMITH
Gaffer. . . . . JOHN G. VELEZ
Best Boy Electric. . . . . DARRIN SMITH
Rigging Gaffer . . . . . . BRIAN PITTS
Best Boy Rigging Electric
. . . . BRENDAN KEEFE
Generator Operator . . LON CARACAPPA
Lamp Operators . . . . . . GEOFF DANN,
                TOM "TK" KENNAN,
        MARK LEWIS, JOHN F. MCPHEE,
                    RYAN RODRIGUEZ

Key Grip . . . . . WILLIAM M. WEBERG
Best Boy Grip . . WARREN A. WEBERG
A Camera Dolly Grip
. . . . TONY CAMPENNI
B Camera Dolly Grip . . . . DAVID LaRUE
Company Grips . . . . JEN EVANS,
        ROBERT KELLY, JEFFREY KING,
                    BILL LeCLAIR
Key Rigging Grip
. . . . DARYL RICHARDSON
Best Boy Rigging Grip
. . . . DAVID PUOPOLO
Property Master . . . . . . DAVID GULICK
Assistant Property Master
. . . . JENNIFER GERBINO
Second Assistant Property Master
. . . . C. KENT LANIGAN
Construction Foremen
. . . . STEPHEN DeBOER
            THEODORE SUCHECKI
Construction Gang Boss
. . . . PAUL WILLIAMSON
Special Effects Supervisor
. . . . STEVE KIRSHOFF
Special Effects Coordinator
. . . . GREG MORELL
Key Special Effects . . . . JUDSON BELL
Special Effects Technician
. . . . ALFREDO CAIRO
2nd 2nd Assistant Director
. . . . DANIELA BARBOSA
DGA Trainee . . . . . . SEAN FARRELL
Key Set PA . . . MICHAEL E. JACOBSON
Set PAs . . . . . CATHERINE FEENEY,
        MARK KILLIAN, HARRY LAPHAM,
        BRAD ROBINSON, BRIANA TAYLOR,
                    NATE WINSLOW
Ms. Binoche's Dialogue Coach
. . . . PEG HALL-PLESSAS
Trainer for Ms. Binoche and Mr. Cook
. . . . AGGIE PERKINS
Storyboard Artist . . . . . . JOHN DAVIS
Assistant to Mr. Hedges . . . TONY SHAFF
Assistant to Mr. Shestack. . JEREMY STEIN
Assistant to Mr. Epstein . . . CONNIE KIM
Assist. to Mr. Shestack & Mr. Epstein
. . . . SHANNON PETRANOFF
Assistant to Ms. Winkler-Ioffreda
. . . . EMILY LYSAGHT
Charge Scenic . . . . . . LEWIS BOWEN
Stand-By Painter . . . . JOE BARILLARIO
Scenic Foreman . . . . DAVID COSTELLO
Scenic Artists . . . . HOPE ARDIZZONE
                KRZYSZTOF J. BRATUN

Greens Coordinator . . PEDRO BARQUIN
Greens Foreman . . . . JEFF DeBELL
Studio Teachers . . . . . . JACQUIE SAUL
KRISTA SELVAGGIO
Studio Teaching Administered By
. . . . ALAN SIMON and
ON LOCATION EDUCATION
Unit Publicist . . . . SCOTT LEVINE
Transportation Coordinator . . MIKE HYDE
Transportation Captain
. . . . ROBERT BUCKMAN
Casting . . . . DAVID VACCARI
WILL CANTLER
Casting Assistants
. . . . STEPHANIE YANKWITT
CHRIS SCHEEREN
Extras Casting
. . . . ANNE MULHALL, LDI CASTING
CAROLYN PICKMAN, CP CASTING, INC.
New York Extras Casting
. . . . GRANT WILFLEY
First Aid . . . . . JACK McCULLOUGH
Catering by
. . . . REEL CHEFS CATERING, LLC
Craft Service . . . . TRACY R. SPIEGEL
Assistant Craft Service . . . . ETHAN FOX
Visual Effects by . . . . . . FURIOUS FX
Visual Effects Supervisor
. . . . DAVID LINGENFELSER
Visual Effects Executive Producer
. . . . SCOTT DOUGHERTY
Visual Effects Producer
. . . . TRACY TAKAHASHI
CG Supervisor . . . . . . MARK SHOAF
Creative Supervisor
. . . . KEVIN LINGENFELSER
Composer . . . . . SEAN O'CONNOR
CG Artists . . . . JOHN BAKER
BRYAN CHAVEZ
CHRIS MacKINNON
Rotoscope Artist . . . . . ERIN CULLEN
Background Vocals
. . . . DAVID KRAMER'S
LOOPING GROUP, GIDEON JACOBS,
CAROLYN MILLER, BRIAN PODNOS,
ALICIA SABLE, MAKAILA ZIMICK
Score Recorded and Engineered by
. . . . . LAWRENCE MANCHESTER,
JASON STASIUM, KATO ÅDLAND,
JØRGEN TRÆEN
Score Mixed by
. . . . . . LAWRENCE MANCHESTER
JASON STASIUM

Orchestrations and Arrangements by
. . . . SONDRE LERCHE
SONNY KOMPANEK
Music Contractor . . . . . SANDY PARK
Assistant to Music Supervisor . . . .
ELIZABETH UMSTEAD
Score Recorded and Mixed at
. . . . LEGACY RECORDING
STUDIOS, NYC, GJØA STUDIO,
DUPER STUDIO
Assistant Engineer . . . . . MISSY WEBB
Digital Intermediate and Opticals by
. . . . TECHNICOLOR®
DIGITAL INTERMEDIATES
A TECHNICOLOR COMPANY
Digital Film Colorist . . SCOTT GREGORY
Digital Intermediate Producer
. . . . CARL MOORE
Digital Edit Conform
. . . . MARK SAHAGUN
Main and End Titles Designed by
. . . . yU+co.
Technicolor® Timer . . . MIKE MERTENS
HD Preview services provided by
. . . . ORBIT DIGITAL
HD Preview Artist . . . . . BRIAN BOYD

SONGS

"AIRPORT TAXI RECEPTION"
Written by Sondre Lerche
Performed by Sondre Lerche and
the Faces Down
Courtesy of Astralwerks
Under license from EMI Film &
Television Music

"THE TAPE"
Written by Sondre Lerche
Performed by Sondre Lerche and
the Faces Down
Courtesy of Astralwerks
Under license from EMI Film &
Television Music

"TO BE SURPRISED"
Written, Produced and Performed by
Sondre Lerche
Mixed by Kato Ådland
Courtesy of EMI/Astralwerks Records

"I'LL BE OK"
Written, Produced and Performed by
Sondre Lerche
Courtesy of EMI/Astralwerks Records

"SEPTEMBER '99" (Phats & Small Remix)
Written by Maurice White, Al McKay and
Allee Willis
Performed by Earth, Wind & Fire
Courtesy of Columbia Records
By arrangement with SONY BMG MUSIC
ENTERTAINMENT

"RUTHIE PIGFACE DRAPER"
Written by Norbert Leo Butz
and Dane Cook
Performed by Dane Cook
and Norbert Leo Butz

"FEVER"
Written by Eddie Cooley
and John Davenport
Produced by Sondre Lerche
Performed by A Fine Frenzy
Courtesy of Virgin Records

"NASTY GIRL"
Written by Prince
Performed by Inaya Day
Courtesy of Star 69 Records/Peppermint
Jam Records
By arrangement with Steel Synch

"HUMAN HANDS"
Written by Elvis Costello
Performed by Sondre Lerche and
the Faces Down Quartet
Courtesy of Astralwerks
Under license from EMI Film &
Television Music

"MY HANDS ARE SHAKING"
Written, Produced and Performed by
Sondre Lerche
Courtesy of EMI/Astralwerks Records

"LET MY LOVE OPEN THE DOOR"
Written by Pete Townshend
Performed by Steve Carell and Dane Cook

"HELL NO"
Written and Produced by Sondre Lerche
Performed by Sondre Lerche and
Regina Spektor
Sondre Lerche appears courtesy of
EMI/Astralwerks Records
Regina Spektor appears courtesy of
Sire Records

"MODERN NATURE"
Written by Sondre Lerche
Performed by Sondre Lerche and Lillian
Samdal
Courtesy of Astralwerks
Under license from EMI Film & Television
Music

Soundtrack Album Available
on Virgin Records

SPECIAL THANKS:
Susan Bruce
Simon Hedges
Kirsten Schatz
The People of Jamestown, RI
The City of Providence, RI
The City of Newport, RI
The Township of Westerly, RI
The Townships of East and
West Greenwich, RI
U.S. Coast Guard Motion Picture Office
CDR Kevin E. Raimer, Director
U.S. Coast Guard Station Point Judith
BMC Patrick C. Foley, Executive
Petty Officer

Artwork courtesy of DAVID LEVINE
Photos courtesy of GETTY IMAGES

With thanks to DOROTHY RAYMOND
and her family

With grateful acknowledgement to the State
of Rhode Island, Governor DONALD L.
CARCIERI, Speaker of the House WILLIAM
J. MURPHY, Senate President JOSEPH A.
MONTALBANO, and STEVEN FEINBERG,
Director, Rhode Island Film & Television
Office.

Copyright © 2007
TOUCHSTONE PICTURES

Distributed By
WALT DISNEY STUDIOS
MOTION PICTURES

About the Filmmakers

Peter Hedges (Director/Co-writer) is a novelist, playwright, screenwriter, and director. He made his feature film directorial debut with *Pieces of April*, starring Katie Holmes, Patricia Clarkson, Oliver Platt, and Derek Luke. The acclaimed film garnered numerous awards, including an Academy Award® nomination for Clarkson. Following the film, *Variety* named Hedges as one of the 10 Directors to Watch in 2003.

Hedges' novel *What's Eating Gilbert Grape* was the basis for the 1993 film, which he also wrote. His second novel, *An Ocean in Iowa*, was published in 1998. His novels have been published in 15 languages. Hedges' screenplay adaptations include Jane Hamilton's *A Map of the World* and Nick Hornby's *About a Boy,* which received a Best Adapted Screenplay Oscar® nomination.

A graduate of the NC School of the Arts, Hedges founded the Edge Theatre in 1985 along with Mary-Louise Parker and Joe Mantello. Over a three-year period he wrote and directed 12 works for the company. Hedges' other plays include "Baby Anger" (Playwrights Horizons), "Good as New" (Manhattan Class Company), and "Imagining Brad" (Circle Repertory Theater), all of which have been published by Dramatists Play Service.

Hedges has taught at Yale University, Bennington College, and the NC School of the Arts. He has served as a Creative Advisor to the Sundance Screenwriters' Lab and has been awarded residencies at Yaddo, the MacDowell Colony, and the Millay Colony. Hedges grew up in West Des Moines, Iowa. He now lives in Brooklyn with his wife, Susan Bruce, and their two children, Simon and Lucas.

Pierce Gardner (Co-writer) was inspired to write *Dan in Real Life* after years of going on summer vacations to Rehoboth Beach, Delaware, with his wife's extended family. Gardner is a native of Pennsylvania and a graduate of Trinity College in Hartford, Connecticut. He began working as a screenwriter in 1996. Currently, he is working on the romantic comedy *Theory of Everything* for Disney and adapting the book *My Korean Deli* for New Line. His first screenplay, the supernatural thriller *Lost Souls*, starring Winona Ryder and Ben Chaplin and directed by Janusz Kaminksi, was made by New Line. Gardner began his film career in production and served as a producer on the MGM comedies *Getting Even with Dad* and *Fatal Instinct*.